STEELE'S WAR:
THE STRANGER

STEELE'S WAR:
THE STRANGER

George G. Gilman

NEW ENGLISH LIBRARY/TIMES MIRROR

For
Phil and Margaret
Be my guests – have a book!

A New English Library Original Publication, 1981

First NEL Paperback Edition September 1981

NEL Books are published by
New English Library Limited,
Barnard's Inn, Holborn,
London EC1N 2JR.

Typeset by Fleet Graphics, Middlesex.

Printed in Finland by
Finland Printers Ltd.

0 450 05250 8

AUTHOR'S NOTE

The Civil War sequence in this book completes the four-part account of Adam Steele's experiences as a cavalry lieutenant in the Confederate army. Although both it and the contemporary story contained in this volume are complete in themselves, enjoyment may be enhanced by reading the earlier three books in the series in chronological order: *The Woman, The Preacher* and *The Storekeeper.*

THE STRANGER: Part One

AFTER the two men out front of the White Rock stage depot had watched the San Antonio bound Concord roll off the single street of the town to head down the south trail, one of them said to the other: 'You know somethin'?'

'What's that?'

'Folks around here are real glad you and your wife decided to stay on at the store. After the trouble.'

Adam Steele smiled quietly and nodded to the stage depot manager whose name was Coburn. And answered: 'Reckon Lucy is, too.'

The chubby-faced Coburn looked slightly perturbed. 'Hope that don't mean *you're* havin' second thoughts, Mr Steele?'

'Never have changed my mind since I bought the store off George Dalton.'

'Folks'll be real glad to hear that,' Coburn said as he turned to go inside the depot, stepping out of the heat and glare of the Texas sun a few minutes past its midday peak.

And Adam Steele angled across the dusty, deserted street toward the White Rock Grocery Store that had provided a home and a living for his wife and himself for almost two months.

At the very start, the omens had been good. When he and his bride had ridden away from a time of violence into this quiet country town on the trail between San Antonio and Abilene: to discover the store up for sale and a bank mortgage readily available. To buy the place and to attempt to put down roots here in White Rock had been an impulsive decision. Just as impulsive as his marriage to Lucy Girard. But then the violence which had surrounded his meeting with the woman and next attended their wedding, intruded yet again. And Adam Steele, storekeeper, was required to revert to being the kind of man whom the War Between the States had moulded and long years of a violent peace had honed.

Although grateful for the way in which the newcomer to White Rock took the brutal initiative in dealing with the trouble that came to their town, the people were shocked by his skill in the killing art and his lack of any feeling toward those who died by his hand. And for some time, Lucy and he could not fail to be aware of the antipathy which the events on the day of the bank robbery had created between the long-standing citizens of White Rock and themselves.

Nothing was said or done directly to make the couple feel they were unwelcome. There was just a subtle change of attitudes among the customers who had to use the store because there was no alternative: a certain coolness that discouraged small town social chitchat and confined conversation to the limit of what was necessary to complete the buying and selling transaction.

Back behind the counter in the cool shade of the store, breathing the air which was redolent with the aromas of his stock in trade, Adam Steele expressed another quiet smile. The period of semi-ostracism was now ended. Coburn had spoken of 'folks around here' being pleased that the Steeles were still working their store in town. And during the morning, before Adam Steele walked his wife across to the depot and saw her on to the stage, a number of women customers had sought assurances that Lucy really was only going to San Antonio to buy a dress for her birthday.

Which meant they had passed some kind of spontaneous test – or, rather, that Steele had been tried and not found wanting. And if he could settle comfortably into the mundane pattern of life in this quiet Texas backwater, then his wife who had not shown herself to be anything but a respectably married woman was equally acceptable to the people of White Rock.

Oddly, she who had done nothing wrong in the eyes of the local people had been most affected by their change of attitude toward Steele: had been moodily anxious for three weeks after the day of the bank robbery for her husband to leave and find a new place to settle down. She had insisted that the reason she wanted this was exclusively on his account – that he was demeaning himself by remaining here, serving an ungrateful community which held him in such low regard.

But Steele was certain this was only partially responsible for her line of thinking – maybe even a pretence – and that there was a deeper, more personal reason for her strong desire to move on. And, certainly, she had stopped trying to convince him they should move on long before this morning, when the people of White Rock had made overtures of renewed friendship toward the couple.

For an hour Steele was alone in the store except for a couple of green-bodied flies which buzzed lethargically in the display window beside the open door. And only for a fraction of this time did he consider why Lucy had changed her mind – or abandoned her attempts to get him to change his. For he did not wish to cloud his mind with unpleasant thoughts and there was too much they did not know about each other: about their respective pasts. Because neither ever asked and information was seldom volunteered. And since Steele was taciturn on this matter because there was so much he did not want Lucy to know, it was natural that he should feel her silence had the same basis.

'A half pound of coffee if you please, young man. I don't suppose you have any eggs?'

His first customer of the afternoon was the thinly-built spinster of advanced years who taught school in town. She had a temperament to match her sour face and so her curt manner was not an indication that she was at odds with the feelings of the rest of the people in White Rock. It was just her way with everyone.

'No eggs,' Steele confirmed, as he placed a package of coffee beans on the counter.

The woman took out the right amount of coins to pay for the coffee and complained: 'You shouldn't allow flies in a store selling provisions, young man.' But then, pausing on the threshold, she glanced back to add in the same tone of voice: 'But you're a fast learner and I am very pleased about that. Good day to you.'

He knew he was a fast learner – especially of those lessons which showed a man how to survive.

During his youth and early manhood, as the son of one of the most wealthy plantation owners in Virginia, this had been easy. First in terms of orthodox school education and then the learning of the social mores and business techniques necessary to fit him for taking over the running of the plantation in due course of time.

But the Civil War made a destructive intrusion into this plan and when, against the wishes of his pro-Union father, the young Adam Steele threw in his lot with the Confederacy, it was not just the war he was destined to lose. He also lost the bright and privileged future which he had always considered his birthright.

The ending of the war marked, for the Virginian, the start of the violent peace when, after cutting down the corpse of his lynched father from a beam in a Washington bar-room, he buried Ben Steele in the grounds of the burnt-out big house and set off to find and punish the killers. He succeeded in this mission by abiding by the lessons of survival which war had taught him: gunning down the murderers with the Colt Hartford rifle which was his sole inheritance from his father.

He still had that rifle, upstairs in a closet of the bedroom he shared with Lucy above the store. It, and a variety of other weapons, had been used on countless occasions to fight his way out of trouble on the many trails he had covered between a madman's fortress in Tennessee and this one street town in Texas. Long, hard trails which had provided few opportunities for him to even think about forgetting those wartime lessons on how a man must kill or be killed.

And through all these years of maintaining a delicate balance on the dangerous line between tense living and brutal dying, he had submitted to the dictates of the ruling fates that marked his course. Until he found Lucy Girard, took her as his wife and ignored the bad omens by calling a halt to his ways as a drifter. Dug in his heels, put his rifle in the closet and defied trouble ever to come his way again.

In truth, it did not. The bank robbery was not his concern, except insofar as he was now a citizen of the town where the raid took place. And it was as a law-abiding citizen that Adam Steele had taken the Colt Hartford from the closet and ridden with the posse in pursuit of the raiders. But when the quarry was tracked down, he was set apart from another storekeeper, the town barber, the stage depot manager, the liveryman, banker and sheriff. For a few violent seconds he was not a storekeeper. He was an avenger with a gun who far outclassed the trio of hard men who had

11

robbed the White Rock bank. And when the acrid gunsmoke cleared, his fellow citizens were appalled by his skill and frightened by the utter lack of compassion which he displayed in the wake of the slaughter.

They were quick to thank him – perhaps for saving their lives – but then had followed the time when they made it plain that they were not so sure they wanted their wives to buy flour and beans from such a man as this.

But now that time was past and throughout the hot afternoon women, some men and a few children came into the store to buy the necessities and some luxuries. Cheerfully smiling and often chattering: never putting into words what Coburn had said, but nevertheless making it clear that Adam and Lucy Steele were welcome additions to White Rock.

At five o'clock, Steele took off his waist apron and went out into the kitchen to wash up and shave. And when he was through, he grinned broadly at his reflection in the broken piece of mirror propped on a shelf above the sink. From the neck down, he knew he looked like a small town storekeeper – even without the apron. For he was dressed in a plain cotton shirt, denim pants and shoes: the clothes spick and span and smelling of the same aromas that clung to the store. Such a garb was far removed from the dudish attire he used to wear, as a throwback to his rich Virginia beginnings, while he was riding the dusty Western trails. And the image that grinned out at him from the looking glass . . . ?

It fitted the clothing.

It was a lean face, lined and tanned to the texture and colour of old leather by continual exposure to the elements. To either side of the coal-black eyes and the gentle mouthline some of the wrinkling suggested that this was the face of a man who had suffered both physically and emotionally, but the evidence was not so pronounced as it once had been, he decided. It was a handsome face, the features regular. With a bone structure that, over the years, had seemed to alter: to manifest the increasing strength of character which had developed within Steele. Above the forehead and down each cheek in long and thick sideburns, his hair no more showed any trace of the auburn it had been when he was young: for premature greyness – he was not yet forty – had now entirely taken over.

'Yeah, I reckon you look the part,' he told his reflection. 'And it doesn't even show how hard you had to work for it.'

He turned and went out of the kitchen, across the store and stepped on to the sidewalk in front: a five and a half foot tall, solidly built man who looked incapable of hurting the two flies still buzzing in the window of his premises. Obviously content with his appearance, his surroundings as he crossed the street in the pale reddish light of the cool evening, and with a chore well done – this chore the not inconsiderable one of moulding himself, under adverse conditions, to merge with such apparent ease into the back-drop of this small town.

'Evenin', Mr Steele,' Bart Dillon greeted brightly as the Virginian crossed the stoop of the saloon and pushed through the batwing doors. 'Usual?'

'Grateful to you.'

Dillon, who was in his late fifties with a once strong body running to fat, owned White Rock's only saloon and hotel. And when necessary pinned a five-pointed star to his shirt front to become the town's part-time sheriff. The bar-room was small, cramped by six chair-ringed tables and a counter which stretched thirty feet along one wall. It was spartan and clean, smelling of tobacco smoke from the pipe of the wan, pallid Felix Humbert who ran White Rock's hardware store. As usual at this hour of the day, Humbert shared with Frank Boyd, the town barber, Riley, the banker, and Grant

Erland, who was the blacksmith and liveryman, a table close to the bar. The four of them drinking beer to settle the dust of the day in their throats and passing the time with a game of penny ante poker.

'Widower for the night, I hear?' the sixty-five year old Miles Riley said with a grin. 'Best we keep an eye on you. Make sure you don't do your lovely little lady wrong.'

Steele responded with a quiet smile to the grins of the card players and to the wink from Bart Dillon as the bartender emerged from a doorway in back of the counter, carrying a steaming mug of black coffee.

On other evenings when Steele had entered the saloon at this time the greetings had never been more than coolly polite. And Miles Riley had refrained at all times since the gunning down of the bank robbers from speaking about Lucy in a way that told of the innocent shine he had taken to her when the Steeles first came to town.

'Still sticking to coffee,' the Virginian pointed out as he raised the mug. 'Anxious that strong liquor will get a hold on me and I might not be able to control the yen I have for Emily Hawkins.'

Grins became gusts of laughter now, as the men conjured up images of the strait-laced and vinegary schoolma'am fending off the sexual advances of a man.

'Have a bottle of rye on the house,' Dillon offered good-humouredly. 'A roll in the hay could be just what that crone needs to improve her disposition.'

'Which'll make a lot of kids hereabouts happy,' Frank Boyd added.

There was another burst of laughter and when this petered out, a horse could be heard on the street. Slow-moving, with weariness discernible in the uneven clop of the hooves.

The card game was resumed, Dillon returned to reading a week old edition of a San Antonio newspaper and Steele sipped at the hot, strong coffee. Low voices and small sounds disturbed the silence, which this evening, was comfortable and totally without strain.

Then the horse was halted outside and the dismounting rider could be heard rasping curses at the animal while he hitched the reins to the rail. His booted feet rapped hard on the stoop boarding and the batwings were thrust forcefully open. Dillon and his five local customers turned to glance with only mild interest at the stranger who entered the saloon so noisily.

'Well, what do you know?' the newcomer growled sourly. 'It ain't a ghost town after all.'

He was in his mid-fifties. Six feet tall and string-bean thin. With an ugly, hollow-cheeked, sunken-eyed face. When he took off his hat to shake trail dust from the brim, his head was seen to be totally bald. A Mexican-style moustache was prominent above and to each side of his small mouth, even though there was at least a three day growth of bristles on his cheeks, jaw and throat. He was dressed in patched and sweat-stained black clothing and carried a Smith and Wesson .44 Russian revolver in a hip holster hung from an ancient gunbelt. There was contempt in his red-rimmed green eyes as he surveyed his surroundings and its inhabitants on his way to the centre of the bar counter.

'Get you somethin'?' Dillon asked.

'Beer for my thirst and a bottle of rye for everythin' else that ails me, mister,' the stranger in town answered. 'Sure is some quiet place this White Rock.'

He put his Stetson back on and rasped the palm of a hand over his bristles while he made another, more careful examination of the men in the saloon.

'Way we like it,' Dillon answered as Steele and the card players ignored the stranger.

A glass of beer was drawn and set down on the counter top. Then a bottle of whiskey and a shot glass were placed

15

beside it. The stranger took the beer at a single swallow through an open gullet, smacked his lips in relish and pushed the shot glass away.

'Why make extra dish washin', mister,' he said, uncorked the whiskey bottle and filled the beer glass brimful with hard liquor. He took the equivalent of three fingers at another single swallow. Then: 'Saw the livery was closed up like most other places in town. That mean I can't get my horse bedded down for the night?'

'Lousy hand anyway,' Grant Erland said, stacked his cards and stood up from the table. 'I'll take care of your mount, stranger.'

'Be warned, mister, he's some mean sonofabitch.'

At the batwings, the liveryman paused to gaze fixedly out over them at the horse hitched to the rail. Then he directed a look of scorn at the travel-stained man standing up to the bar. And rasped: 'If someone treated me as bad as that animal's been handled, don't reckon I'd be too even tempered.'

'Just want the beast bedded down, liveryman,' the stranger answered coldly without turning to look at Erland. 'Ain't intendin' to enter him in no prettiest horse contest.'

Grant Erland's exit was as forceful as the stranger's entrance had been.

'You want to take Grant's chair for awhile, Steele?' Felix Humbert invited.

'Why not?' the Virginian agreed as he moved to the table.

'Why not indeed,' Riley echoed. 'I'm sure your charming wife would not consider that you taking a hand in such a small stakes game would also constitute taking advantage of her absence?'

'You know something?' the Virginian drawled reflectively as he sat down and Frank Boyd began the deal. 'I don't think Lucy even realises I know how to play poker.'

Not until after he had picked up his five cards and made a

fan of them was he aware of being an object of intense concentration. And raised his own coal-black eyes to meet the stare of emnity directed at him by the green ones of the stranger. For just part of a second the two gazes remained locked.

Then the stranger switched his attention to Dillon and asked: 'You got a room for rent, mister?'

'Sure. How long for?'

'Just tonight.'

'I'll show you up there when you're ready.'

'Won't be until after I've had my supper, mister,' the stranger growled, raising the whiskey bottle to emphasise what he meant. Then topping up the beer glass with rye, 'Is there a whore in this town?'

Bart Dillon, who had responded to the man's surly manner with impassiveness, now frowned. 'I don't allow loose women to operate in White Rock, stranger.'

'*You* don't allow?'

Steele asked Boyd for two cards and failed to fill a long shot flush, but had three queens with a wild deuce. He supplied: 'Dillon's our sheriff, feller.'

'When it's necessary that we need a lawman in town,' the man behind the bar counter added. 'Which ain't often.'

The stranger looked hard at Dillon, then nodded and growled: 'Now I recognise you, mister.'

'You do? I ain't never seen you before. Far as I know.'

'You wouldn't have. Same as them four playin' cards and the big guy that went to take care of my horse. On account of I only ever seen all of you in a picture at a show over in New Orleans. This here picture.'

The card game was curtailed as all the players directed their attention toward the stranger, who took a crumpled envelope from a hip pocket, carefully extracted a photograph from it and smoothed out its creases on the counter top before turning it for Dillon to look at, right way up.

17

Dillon bent low over the picture.

And a moment later the bartender's flabby features were lit with a bright smile and he beckoned to the men at the table. 'Hey, come look at this. It's one of them pictures that crazy kid photographer took the day the bank was robbed. Just before the posse took off after the three that hit the bank.'

Riley, Boyd and Humbert hurried to get up from the table while Dillon yelled at Erland who had re-entered the saloon followed by Coburn – telling these two what had caused the excitement. Steele made less haste to join the group gathering at the bar: conscious of being closely scrutinised again by the stranger. Who had backed off a few feet with his big glass of whiskey to allow the men a clear view of the picture.

'Well, I'll be,' Boyd blurted and giggled.

'Look at that, if it ain't the whole bunch of us outside my place,' Erland added.

'I'd completely forgotten about that young man taking pictures,' Riley put in. 'What was his name?'

'Crenshaw,' Dillon supplied. 'Look, it says his name underneath.'

'Hey, he took a whole bunch, didn't he?' Coburn recalled. 'Not just that day. He was here awhile. Was gonna write a book if I remember right.'

'He's doing that now,' the stranger confirmed, his interjection bringing the excited chatter to a halt as Steele reached the bar and craned his neck to see the picture. Although it was badly stained and crinkled from being carried in the stranger's pocket, the definition was clear enough for the faces of the subjects to be recognised. The seven men now looking at it, seen astride horses in front of Erland's livery stable: formed into a posse which moments after the photograph was taken set out northwards from White Rock to track down the bank raiders. With, in the

18

background, Lucy Steele come to a sudden halt in the middle of the street, an expression of deep fear marring her pretty face. A look which, so far, only her husband had noted.

'It was said so at the show where I stole the picture from,' the stranger went on, his attention still concentrated on the Virginian. 'Lots of others pictures there. One showing how things ended up after you men caught the ones that robbed the bank. And it was said about how the pictures was from a whole lot this Crenshaw took. For some kinda book he was gonna do about what it's like to live in a town out West.'

'Ain't you got the other picture?' Coburn asked eagerly, unaware like most of the others in the group that there was a sudden tension in the attitude of the stranger.

'No mister. Wasn't nothin' of interest to me in that one. Just three dead men and a couple of you lookin' at them.'

'What do you find so interesting in this one?' Miles Riley asked tautly, and was the first to realise that Steele was the cause of the stranger's tenseness.

'The woman,' was the curt response.

Now all eyes were shifted to look at the Virginian. And booted feet scraped floorboards as the group split to leave open space between the stranger and the storekeeper. Even though Steele's impassiveness revealed nothing of what he was thinking. And there was no aggression in the manner of the other man.

'What about her, feller?' the Virginian asked evenly.

'Heard you mention your wife's name is Lucy, mister?'

'You heard right.'

'That's her right there in the picture,' Frank Boyd supplied, and then looked innocently contrite under withering stares from some of his fellow citizens.

'Always was a chance of there being two women named Lucy, even in a town this size,' the stranger said. 'Or that one in the picture was just passin' through the day it was took.'

'I asked what about her, feller?' Steele repeated and, although his face was still just a mask of blankness, ice had crept into his tone.

'I don't want any trouble!' Bart Dillon growled. 'In this saloon or this town.'

'What about her, mister? She ain't your wife.'

Steele's throat felt dry. Then it was moist and he tasted bile in his mouth. No questions asked and no lies invited and told. That had been the unspoken agreement between them. It had worked fine until now, except for that day of the bank robbery. When Steele had asked Lucy why she was afraid of the young Crenshaw. And had been told she had mistaken him for someone she used to know. The future had been bright and settled. Today had seemed to set the seal on this. Now this emaciated, embittered stranger was on the brink of destroying it. And the decent men who had accepted him in their midst were once more afraid of Adam Steele. Who, in the electric silence of the twilit saloon, looked not at all like a small town storekeeper while he struggled against physical sickness and emotional upheaval in the face of the stranger's bald statement.

Stretched seconds were sliced off the present to slide into the past. Then Steele swallowed hard and his voice was husky when he asked: 'You want to tell me why that is, feller?'

'My name's King, mister. Harry King. Mean anythin' to you?'

'No.'

The stranger who now had a name blew out some air between pursed lips. 'How about Girard?'

'Her maiden name, uh?'

King nodded.

'What's this all about?' Boyd wanted to know.

Dillon glared at him.

But Riley supplied: 'Way it sounds, Frank, Mrs Steele can't really be Mrs Steele in law. Because, if this stranger is to be believed, she married him first.'

'Way it sounds is the way it is,' King confirmed.

'Well, I'll be!' Boyd gasped. Then joined most of his fellow citizens in directing pitying looks toward the Virginian.

'You didn't know,' King said and his inflection added no query.

Steele turned to face the bar and hooked both hands over its front edge. 'Pour me a rye, Dillon,' he instructed.

'But you don't drink nothin' stronger than coffee!'

'Medicinal, feller.'

'If you want to hear the whole story, mister, you'll maybe feel like drinkin' a whole distillery. In celebration.'

The Virginian shuddered, and tightened his grip on the bar. So that his knuckles showed white through the elements-stained skin.

'Easy, Steele,' Dillon warned.

The two men clashed eyes across the counter top and just for part of a second the bigger, older man saw the killer glint in those of the Virginian.

Then Steele was impassive again. And his tone was even when he said: 'A celebration it is then. Give everyone a drink.'

'You don't have to do . . . ' Miles Riley started.

'I know I don't,' Steele cut in and a grim smile spread across his face. 'So it's real big o' me, isn't it?'

STEELE'S WAR
Book Four

CHAPTER ONE

LIEUTENANT Adam Steele was sick at heart and attempting the age old remedy of drowning his depressions in drink.

It was the mid-November of 1863 and for the third time that year he was with a part of the Confederate Army of America that had a fine opportunity to strike a hard and perhaps decisive blow at the Yankees. But in his present mood of morose dejection the young Rebel cavalry officer had scant faith in the ability of his superiors to take advantage of the situation.

He had been at Chancellorville in May when the Confederacy won the battle, but gained nothing of long-term strategic importance from victory. And he was there at Gettysburg in July, riding behind Jeb Stuart, as full of optimism as most other Rebel soldiers that they would all follow General Robert E Lee himself into the city of Washington. There to force Abe Lincoln to sue for peace. But that battle had turned out to be a humiliating disaster for the Confederacy. And with drunken hindsight, the young Steele was certain there never had been a snowball's chance in hell of the Army of Northern Virginia beating the Union's Army of the Potomac.

Because Lee, Stuart, Longstreet and every other damn general in the Rebel army were nothing but a bunch of incompetents: who either lost battles through their feeble-minded bumblings or were so surprised when they won that they were rendered impotent to grasp the initiative and follow through.

Which was going to happen here in the mountains around Chattanooga.

'No doubt about it,' Steele slurred.

'What'd you say, Lieutenant?' a woman asked.

Steele raised his head from where it had been resting on his folded arms and blinked several times to get his liquor-glazed eyes to focus on his surroundings. Saw first the face of the woman, then the dimly lit lamp that hung from the ceiling above the table where they sat. Next the shadowy shapes of furniture in the small room. And within a few moments, as his head began to thud in a painful rhythm and the mixed stinks of body sweat and stale liquor assaulted his nostrils, he recalled precisely where he was and why he was there: his fully awake mind extending the line of thought that was triggered in those confused seconds before he roused from the drunken stupor.

He was in a two-room shack on a piece of high ground in eastern Georgia called Lookout Mountain. To the south-east of Chattanooga which was across the state line in Tennessee. In that city, after being beaten in the bloody Battle of Chickamauga, was the entire Union Army of the Cumberland. For almost a month General Braxton Bragg's Confederate Army of Tennessee had kept the Yankees tightly bottled in Chattanooga intent, by all accounts, on starving them into surrender.

But Bragg was maybe the most incompetent general of the whole bunch. For while he waited with his men positioned on Lookout Mountain, Missionary Ridge to the east and Orchard Knob to the north, the Union high command succeeded in opening up a rail and river supply line into the city. And along this route came not only rations and ammunition for the recently beaten army: but also reinforcements.

Soon, therefore, the Yankees would be in a position to launch a counter-offensive and so Bragg and his most senior officers had adopted a new strategy: as negative as the first had been. They had failed to starve the Union army into surrender during a period when they could have carried out a decisive assault on the city and the demoralised soldiers who held it. Now they waited on the rugged high ground, intending to defend their positions against an attack by a bluebelly army that was getting larger and stronger with each hour that elapsed.

'What?' he asked of the woman who was at least twice his age of twenty-six.

'You said somethin'.' She was tall and thin, dressed in a ragged and filthy once white dress that hung shapelessly on her bony frame. She had grey hair and a time-worn face that, in the dim light of the lamp, showed faint traces of a classic beauty she had possessed in years gone by. 'If it was more moonshine you was askin' for, it's all gone.'

Steele forced himself to his feet by pressing with both hands on the table. He made it, but his chair tipped over backwards.

'You leavin'?' the woman asked, suddenly anxious. 'The girl oughta be back most any time now.'

'Need some air,' Steele told her and had to concentrate hard on placing one foot in front of the other as he went to the door. There dragged it open and leaned against the frame while he took several deep breaths.

It was pitch-black beyond the fringe of the light from the doorway and a gentle rain was falling. The night was advancing toward the dawn and the mountain air of the Cumberland Plateau was chill – served to revive and refresh the lean of stature, weakly handsome young man who rubbed the back of a gloved hand over the stubble on his jaw and began to hate himself. This as, from the north, came the crackle of rifle fire.

Orchard Knob was under attack. Or maybe the Yankees had already taken it and were now mopping up the final pockets of Rebel resistance. Men had died and were still dying out there on another hilltop. While Adam Steele, who considered himself a better tactician than every general in the CSA, got drunk on cheap whiskey, lusted for a whore and felt sick to his stomach as he reflected in this pre-dawn time on what he was doing here.

'You have any coffee in this place, ma'am?' he asked when he had breathed in enough of the cold, fresh, wet air to fight the bile back down his throat.

'Surely. You come sit down and I'll start some. Maybe by the time it's ready, the girl will be back.'

Steele closed the door and returned to the table, while the woman went to the stove in the corner to light the kindling and begin fixing a pot of coffee.

He sat down and watched her for a few moments. Then stared at the backs of his gloved hands spread on the table. He had seen no action since the Gettysburg debacle almost five months ago. Which just about summed up how his war had gone – long periods of frustrating inactivity begun and ended with explosions of fierce fighting. In which he acquitted himself well, learned whatever lessons the experiences taught him, but felt cheated of any reward.

Which was not how he had imagined war would be when, after a bitter quarrel with his father, he left the Steele Plantation to follow a group of his friends to Richmond – there to enlist in the Rebel army. Like those friends, and tens of thousands of other young men who flocked to answer the call of President Jefferson Davis, Adam Steele's mind had been filled with heady thoughts of honour and glory as he played his role in winning victory for the Southern Cause under the waving banners of the Stars and Bars.

Gradually, disillusionment had set in: relieved from time to time by periods of cynicism as he faced up to inevitable defeat and became determined to win his private war by setting himself the simple objective of survival. Mostly of late he had been able to sustain such an attitude and his morale in the wake of the Gettysburg defeat had been high. And had remained so when his troop was detached from Lee's Army of Northern Virginia and sent west for reassignment to Bragg's Army of Tennessee.

The battle had been lost, but he had emerged from it unscathed. And in prospect was the strong possibility of seeing a large part of the Union army lay down its weapons to stagger into captivity. But as the rainy days and nights went by and the tension of confrontation eased, Steele was again visited by demoralising disenchantment occasioned by boredom.

And he began to think about his father who was committed to the Union cause. A man whose every word about the outcome of the war was going to be proved correct. He reflected, too, upon those friends from the Virginia town of Keysville whom he followed to Richmond. Banning and Davidson, Conrad Shotter and Andy Harding. Nick Kane and Cliff Gordon. Gordon – more an enemy than a friend – had survived Gettysburg but was likely to be dead now after some small skirmish that history would fail to record. As dead as those other men who had been kids around Keysville at the same time as Steele.

Diana? It was thinking of her that had brought the young lieutenant to this shack high on the mountain. A shack where the well-founded rumour had it a man could get drunk and bed a woman while he waited to kill or be killed.

The girl had been away from the place when Steele reached it after a long climb on foot up the mountain. Gone, her widowed mother explained, to the quarters of a general who was unable to leave his command post. And Steele began to drink the moonshine while he waited, only half-listening to the widow woman's tale of woe. Of how her husband was killed at Vicksburg and she and her daughter had been unable to keep body and soul together, working the poorly cropping fields around the shack during the time he had been away never to return. So the daughter had taken to whoring in Chattanooga while her mother brewed the rotgut whiskey. But the girl had left the city after the Battle of Chickamauga. Since the siege had started mother and daughter had been forced to endure the greatest shame of all – turning their farmstead into a brothel.

The more liquor Steele poured down his throat, the less attention he paid to the droning voice of the woman. And the more his lust for her absent daughter increased. While he wondered how she would compare with Diana Summers. The girl he had asked to marry him just a day before he left to take up arms for the South. Only she was no longer Diana Summers. For she was now married to a lawyer and living in Baltimore. Which meant that an unseen whore held more promise for him than did the woman who had once agreed to be his wife.

The moonshine took its effect and he slid into a stupor, during which the grim realities of the past became nightmares. Filling his mind with irrational images until he was on the brink of awareness: when he sought again to blame his disillusionment on the way the war was fought from the top.

'Here you are, lieutenant. Hot and strong. On the house. You just owe me two dollars for the liquor.'

She set down the mug of coffee between his splayed

hands and he thanked her with a nod of his head as he picked it up with both hands and sipped the fresh brew. It scalded his mouth and throat and before it hit his stomach he thought it was going to come up again. But it stayed and with each sip the feeling of nausea grew less. The distant gunfire from the north became more sporadic.

'I'm real sorry,' the woman said as she sat down across the table from him again.

He looked at her and saw her more clearly now: realised this was because the first grey light of the new day was filtering through the window to augment the glow of the lamp. She looked older than he remembered, and haggard to the point of ugliness. And he smelled her – the stink worse than that which emanated from his own pores and mouth.

'For what, ma'am?'

'Spillin' out my troubles to you. For you surely have plenty of your own. Like most folks in this war. On whichever side.'

'Reckon no one will give you an argument about that.' He delved into a pocket of his uniform tunic and brought out a five dollar bill which he dropped to the table.

'You want me to make change, or keep it to cover the price of goin' with the girl?'

'Keep it.'

She crumpled the bill in a clawed fist and pushed it into a pouch at the waist of the loose-fitting dress.

Rain rattled harder on the roof and windows of the shack. Then, moments later, the sound was masked by the crackle of rifle fire: which briefly swelled in volume as the door of the place was flung open and slammed closed.

'We gotta leave, Ma! We gotta leave right away!'

The girl sagged against the door, eyes closed and body trembling as she yelled the words between gasping for breath.

31

'What's the matter, girl?'

Steele was on his feet, straining his ears to try to judge the distance over which the gunfire was coming: and more eager than the woman to hear her daughter's response.

'The Yankees are comin'! They said not until tomorrow, but they're comin' now!'

The woman stared in terror at the young lieutenant as comprehension swept the look of curiosity off his face. Then she got fast to her feet and swung her head to glare at the girl.

'We got company, Matty,' she said, struggling to disguise the fact that it was a warning.

The gunfire which had sounded as the girl burst into the shack was over. It had been triggered from relatively close by. And now there was a fiercer and constant barrage which reached up the mountainside from the foot of the slope.

Matty opened her eyes. Green eyes set in a face that bore a striking family resemblance to that of the old woman. A once-beautiful face that had been marred by a tragic amount of hard living packed into her less than twenty years.

'It was the Rebels told me!' she blurted, after twice swallowing hard in an attempt to swamp the fear that showed in every line of her pallid, dissipated face and every fibre of her slender, trembling body. 'They said them stinkin' bluebellies wouldn't hit until tomorrow!'

Matty was a Union spy. From the moment she had gasped out a reply to her mother's demand, Adam Steele had never been more sure of anything in his life. Her father and the woman's husband might well have been killed at Vicksburg, but fighting for which side? The whole family was one of many in the Cumberland Mountains that favoured the Yankee cause – the well-known sympathies of the area in and around Chattanooga being a prime reason for the Union's offensive move into it.

Steele unfastened his holster and fisted a gloved hand around the butt of the Dance Brothers revolver nestling in it. Matty's mother, too. They had the perfect cover for gaining intelligence on Rebel strength and plans to pass to the Yankees. The girl with her body and the mother with her bathtub liquor.

The rain beat harder than ever against the shack and the continuous rattle of far off gunfire also intruded into the tense, sweating silence that was trapped between the walls. Then came shouted words:

'There it is!'

'Surround the place!'

'Keep your heads down!'

'And your mouths shut!'

Steele drew the revolver from the holster and felt sick to his stomach again: as he saw the fear of dying become inscribed deeper into the faces of the mother and daughter.

'Ma!' Matty cried, and seemed to try to push away from the door. But was rooted to the spot.

While her mother looked as if she might be on the point of attempting to back the girl's pathetically obvious lie. Then covered her face with her hands for a moment, before clasping them at her breasts in an attitude of prayer.

'We never asked for no war, lieutenant,' she explained with soft sincerity. 'How many ordinary folks like you and us did? But when it come, we had to do what we could to stay alive. You can understand that, son. Can't you?' Tears spilled from her deep-set eyes as Steele looked at her without compassion and swung the revolver to aim it at Matty. 'It's what we was gettin' in to talk about before my little girl came back.'

'No use staying alive unless you have respect for yourself, ma'am,' Steele said coldly, swept his gaze toward the point where the gun was aimed. And squeezed the trigger.

As the son of a wealthy Virginia landowning family,

33

Adam Steele had been familiar with gunsports since he was old enough and strong enough to hold and fire a rifle or shotgun. And he was a fine marksman with such weapons. He had scant regard for revolvers but had grown accustomed to carrying one and using it during the war. But even had he not fired one before, it would have been difficult for him to miss the target over such a short range in his present mood of grim determination.

It was intended as a heart shot and the bullet tunneled into Matty's flesh beneath her small left breast to find and destroy the vital organ. For what seemed a great many stretched seconds, the girl remained alive and upright: as solid and rigid against the door as the revolver was firm in the fist of her killer. Then her mouth gaped wide, her eyes glazed over and she slid down the door to form an inert heap on the floor.

'May your soul burn forever in the fires of hell!' the woman shrieked. And clawed her hands to hook her fingers over the neckline of her dress and rip the fabric.

'The bitches are shootin' at us!' a man out front of the shack yelled.

'Fire! Pour it in, men!' This command roared from the side of the place.

A volley of shots exploded, to mask the sounds of the beating rain and the battle taking place on the lower slopes of Lookout Mountain. Bullets thudded into timber walls and shattered windows, showering glass shards across the floor.

Steele swung his revolver and his gaze toward the mother of the dead girl. And just for a moment was disconcerted by the sight of her flaccid, elongated breasts bared to his eyes. But then he saw that her action was not part of some half-crazed display of grief – that her scrawny hands were struggling to free a tiny gun from the folds of her filthy underwear.

34

Any one of several bullets that gained entrance to the room could well have felled either or both of the two people facing each other across the table. But both were spared, so that destiny forced Steele to kill again in a matter of seconds. Cocking the hammer of the Dance Brothers and triggering a shot into the bared flesh of the old woman an instant before she could fire the Remington over-and-under aimed at him.

She staggered backwards and dropped on to the chair where she had sat for most of the night, urging Steele to drink more moonshine while she listened intently for whatever scrap of useful military information a mere cavalry lieutenant might unwittingly reveal with a liquor-loosened tongue. And as she did so, her arms jerked and the small derringer was tossed involuntarily into the air. Steele caught the gun with his free hand at the instant the woman died – teetered for a moment on the chair, then tipped to the side and slid to the floor.

Only then, a gun held in each gloved hand, did the Virginian go to the floor himself: diving hard and pressing himself flat as the men on every side of the shack intensified their shooting in response to the second gunshot from inside. For long moments he stayed immobile, arms over his head and every muscle in his body tensed in expectation of a ricochetting bullet tearing into his flesh. Then there was a pause in the onslaught. And he could hear that the rain had eased. But that the battle lower down the mountain was coming closer.

'You men outside!' he yelled.

'Hold your fire!' one of them bellowed. 'Cease fire! There's a guy in there!'

'A bluebelly most likely! Come to see what the whore's found out!'

'She's dead!' Steele shouted. 'And her mother, too! I'm Lieutenant Steele, CSA Cavalry! I'm coming out!'

He remained on his belly on the floor until the obvious commander of the men surrounding the shack ordered: 'Do like I say and hold your fire! If he ain't who he says he is, he won't have his hands way above his head when he shows himself!'

Steele got to his feet now, put on his uniform cap and went to the door: had to drag the corpse of the girl out of the way before he could ease it open. Then, with a gun in each hand, he raised his arms high and stepped out into a morning that was lanced with rain and layered with mist.

'He's wearing the right uniform, Sergeant!' a disembodied voice allowed from out of the gently moving mist.

'Hold it right there, mister!' a man called from another direction.

Steele did as he was told, and heard rustling foliage and booted feet crossing over muddy ground. Then moved his eyes in their sockets to spot each shadowy figure that emerged from the greyness. Seven of them, advancing in an arcing line with .58 Springfield carbines levelled from the hip. All of them infantrymen. A sergeant and six privates. Wearing sodden, mud-spattered uniforms.

'My apologies, sir,' the non-com said abruptly, lowering his carbine and throwing up a fast salute. 'But a soldier can't be too careful when there are enemy agents about.'

Steele nodded and then directed a glance at three men who were still aiming carbines at him: did not lower his arms and speak before these had removed the threat.

'You did the right thing, sergeant. It sounds like we're under attack below?'

'Got caught like sittin' ducks,' the oldest of the privates said sourly.

'That's right, sir,' the black-bearded sergeant confirmed. 'The Yankees came swarmin' up the hill out of the mist and rain with no warnin'. And we couldn't do nothin' else but

36

fall back.'

'But we ain't runnin' away, sir,' a young, frightened-looking private hastened to add.

'That's right, sir,' the sergeant said again. 'We was ordered to come up here and get the whore and her Ma. By Captain Haskins. Seems the girl spent the night in some general's tent, sir. We weren't told which general. And after she'd gone this general found out she'd been goin' through his papers. That's when the Yankees started comin' up the hill at us. Me and these boys were closest when Captain Haskins got the order to go after the whore and her Ma. Capture them and bring them back. Or kill them.'

'You can report back that they're both dead, sergeant,' Steele said.

The bearded face of the non-com clouded with indecision. Then, without meeting Steele's gaze, he started: 'It ain't that I dis . . . '

The Virginian stepped away from the threshold of the shack, holstering his revolver and pushing the over-and-under into a pocket of his uniform tunic. 'Never report as fact anything you don't know for sure is so,' he said. 'Take a look.'

He tilted his head back to get the full refreshing effect of the rain hitting his face: hopeful it would help to diminish the numbness of too much liquor and ease the depression following the murder of two women – executed for doing what they considered to be their duty.

But ever since he had emerged from the shack, heavy artillery fire had been sounding from lower down the mountain. And whatever pleasant effect the cool rain might have had was negated by the acrid taint of exploded black powder which was carried in the misty morning air.

The sergeant said: 'Much obliged, sir. They're both dead sure enough. Am I able to tell Captain Haskins how it was you came to kill them, lieutenant?'

'Same reason why so many people are dying right now, sergeant. They were on one side and I was on another.'

'Sure, sir.' The bearded man saluted again. 'Reckon the captain will be glad enough to know the whore's dead. The details of how it happened ain't important, seems to me.' He swung away and snapped: 'Right, you men. Let's get back down this damn mountain.'

They started to move away from the shack while Steele held back a moment. To glance inside at the two slumped bodies. 'Couple of details are important to me, feller,' he muttered. 'Paid for the liquor I drank. And the whore I nailed instead of screwed.'

CHAPTER TWO

THE short-lived fight in which the Union forces streamed out of Chattanooga and swarmed up Lookout Mountain to inflict another humiliating defeat on the Confederacy was to be termed the Battle above the Clouds by the newspapers.

And to Lieutenant Adam Steele and other survivors in both blue and grey uniforms it was a description which they could go along with – in part. For a great deal of the fighting took place on the high ground, up on the mountain top that was humped above the morning mist. But it was not so much a battle as a rout, the Rebels entrenched on the slopes taken totally by surprise at the speed with which the once besieged and near starving Yankees came out of the city and rushed the high ground.

The Virginian and the detail of infantrymen commanded by the black-bearded sergeant never did get back to their respective positions after leaving the shack with the two dead women slumped inside. And were well short of the objectives when the front-runners of the retreating soldiers came through the mist at them.

Cannons roared, shells burst, small-arms crackled, bullets

cracked, men yelled and screamed and wept, horses snorted and wagons creaked. The air stank of gunsmoke, human waste, the sweat of fear and the indefinable smell of fresh blood. The awful sounds, horrifying sights and the evil smells of front line war assaulted the sense of Adam Steele once again. And once again he threw himself into the fighting with total detachment from the overall purpose and outcome of the bedlam on all sides of him. Determined to survive with honour whether in victory or defeat and, when it was possible, to assist his comrades in arms to stay alive.

He could have attained this simply by turning tail and joining the leaders of the retreat – up to the crest of Lookout Mountain and then down the far side. And had he been at the rear of the Confederate positions when the attack came, this is doubtless what he would have done. But that had not been the case. While his troop commander and the troopers were resting in camp, Steele had climbed the hill, to get drunk and wait for an opportunity to go with a woman. And, although this was simply a matter of bad timing which could not have been forseen, he felt duty-bound to make amends for what he regarded as an act of irresponsibility.

So, carrying a Spencer carbine confiscated from a man with a bullet-shattered shoulder, he pressed on against the tide of grey-uniformed figures plunging up the craggy, brush-covered slope. And did not begin to move with the mass until he saw a teenage corporal pitch to the ground and display two blood-blossoming wounds in the centre of his back.

The shots which sent the young non-com to a sprawling death in a patch of lush green grass were fired from a clump of timber some sixty feet away.

'Another good Rebel!' a man yelled in triumph as he and a second blue-uniformed figure burst out of the trees at a fast run.

Steele had started to turn when the corporal fell. But now he held his position and simply dropped into a crouch in the insubstantial cover of some low-growing brush. Where he laid the carbine on the sodden ground and drew the Dance Brothers handgun from his holster: held his breath and waited until the two Yankees were level with him. Then, without giving the men any kind of warning, he began to fan the hammer of the revolver with his finger curled to the trigger.

The range was less than fifteen feet and the closest man died without knowing what had happened. The other one had time to turn his head and see Steele crouched in the brush. But could do no more than glower his rage before the bullets tore into his flesh and ripped fatal wounds in a vital organ.

A moment after this man was an inert heap on the ground, a barrage of cannon fire filled the world with a deafening roar. Which was ended with the individual crashes of the shells exploding. And Steele was sent flat to the ground by the blast – managed to haul himself over on to his belly and cover his head with his arms before debris began to rain down on and around him.

When it was over, his ears still drumming with the echo of the gunfire inside his head, he opened his eyes and saw a dismembered hand and a booted foot caught in the brush only inches away from his face. Then glanced through the drifting smoke of the explosions to see there was just a hole in the ground where the two Union men had fallen.

'What a lousy waste,' he growled as he grabbed the Spencer and pushed to his feet. 'Of ammunition.'

The Union cannon barrage had acted to stall the advance of the Yankee infantry and Steele had time to double-back up the mountain slope. To escape from the temporary no-man's-land created by the heavy guns and join the stragglers of the retreating Rebels. Time, too, to ask questions of the

41

embittered and demoralised men. The answers to which eventually led him to the edge of a small lake where the survivors of his troop were gathered.

There were not many of them and the sense of satisfaction he had derived from gunning down the two Yankees at such close range – which had been diminishing with every dispirited Rebel soldier he had seen – was finally negated completed as he came around a slab-like rock and saw the remnants of D Troop, which had ground to an exhausted halt on the shingle beach beside the gently rippling grey water.

'Mr Steele, sir, am I glad to see you,' Sergeant Grady yelled as he rose to his feet beside the supply wagon which seemed to be still intact. 'Captain Tyson's in a real bad way.'

A half dozen troopers who had been sprawled or squatting on the beach in the rain also came upright. Nine others remained where they were. Maybe two dozen saddle horses showed not the slightest interest in the arrival of the lieutenant. Tyson was able to raise his head briefly and glance with something akin to envy at Steele as the Virginian came to a halt at the side of the wagon and dropped to his haunches to look beneath it – where the litter on which the captain lay had been placed to keep the rain off him.

'Sorry I'm late, sir. The troop took some finding.'

'The Yankees had no trouble at all,' the forty-year-old, built like an ox, regular service officer rasped as his head fell back on the folded raincape that served as a pillow.

Steele felt a surge of anger at the implied criticism in the captain's tone. For it was Tyson who had suggested his lieutenant take some time out for a little recreation at the shack of the two women: after visiting it several times himself. And the Virginian was on the point of reminding the man of this, and further excusing his absence by revealing what Matty and her mother really had been. But was grateful when the grim-faced Sergeant Grady squatted down beside him and said: 'We got caught in the first attack, Mr Steele. Lost twelve men dead and the captain took two bullets in the belly before the rest of us had a chance to fire a shot. Beat back the bastards for awhile, but then got the order to pull out.'

The Virginian had already seen the dark staining on the blanket at the point where it covered the captain's mid-section. Now saw that Tyson had squeezed his eyes closed and was gritting his teeth in response to a fresh wave of pain that was emanating from the bloodied wounds.

'What's done is done,' the dying man hissed through his clenched teeth and each word caused a stricture to tremor his right cheek. 'And it won't be long until I'm just something that used to be. So listen, lieutenant and listen good. The order to withdraw wasn't the only one that came after the Union hit us.'

His hands moved under the blanket but the effort triggered more pain. Too much. And moisture gleamed in his eyes.

'Damn it, I can't do a lousy thing. In my breast pocket, mister. Sealed orders from General Bragg's headquarters. Take the troop east and pray you get across Missionary Ridge before the Union hit our boys there hard as they have on this mountain. Far east as the Western and Atlantic Railroad. When you reach the tracks, open the orders and follow them. Guess that's clear enough, mister?'

'It's clear, sir.'

'Fine. So move out. Leave the wagon and me. You don't want to be burdened with anything that'll slow you down.'

'Get to it, sergeant,' Steele told the thirty-year-old tall and rangy Grady. 'Have the men take whatever supplies they can reasonably carry from the wagon. Then mount them.'

'Yes, sir.'

43

The non-com moved off and began to relay the orders. This as Steele raised the blanket covering the badly wounded captain and delved gently in one of his pockets to draw out a stout but unbulky envelope sealed with wax. There was no address on the envelope.

'Lieutenant?' Tyson said softly as the blanket was replaced over his chest.

'Sir?'

'Those women have something for what ailed you last night?'

The rain fell softly, the water of the lake rippled and gurgled on the beach, the troopers made only small sounds as they prepared to leave and there was just an occasional exchange of gunfire in the distance. But the atmosphere was oppressive with misery on this patch of mountain above the clouds. And it was easy for Steele to consider that Captain Tyson, his pain numbed and on the brink of death, was the only man clad in Confederate grey who was able to smile. At remembered pleasures and in expectation of vicarious joy.

'They sure did, sir,' he reported and forced a smile to his own lips, in pretence of reflecting on an interlude of satisfying liquor-boosted lust.

Tyson sighed. 'That's good,' he murmured dreamily. 'In war, a man has to take what he can of the good things of life while they're going, lieutenant. I remember a night in the Peninsular Campaign. Woman in Mechanicsville. Me and another kid lieutenant. Stupid sonofabitch drank so much he couldn't raise it. Next day at Gaines Mill he got it shot off. Proves something, wouldn't you say?'

'Reckon so, sir.'

'Like keep your pecker up – except when there's lead flying.'

He began to laugh at his own joke. The laughter became a coughing fit. A strangled word was vented from the man's gaping mouth and, whatever it was, it was the last one Tyson ever spoke. Blood bubbled up from his throat and he lay still. And when the blood had ceased to trickle from a corner of his mouth there was nothing about him that moved.

Steele got to his feet and pushed the sealed orders into a pocket of his own tunic.

'The captain dead, sir?' Grady asked as he moved away from the rear of the wagon.

'Reckon it was better than to stay alive with a gut injury, sergeant.'

The morose-faced non-com nodded and vented a soft sigh. 'Sounded as if he died happy, sir.'

'He was a good trooper,' Steele drawled as he buttoned the pocket in which the orders were resting. 'Left us laughing.'

CHAPTER THREE

THEY left Tyson where he had died on the litter beneath the supply wagon and moved off from the lakeside. Fifteen troopers, a sergeant and a lieutenant. Down into the valley, across a creek that was a tributary of the Tennessee River and up the other side to go over the crest of Missionary Ridge. Where the entrenched Rebels who still held this piece of high ground gazed sourly westwards: at the Union flag that now fluttered limply from a pole atop Lookout Mountain.

D Troop rode with their topcoats on against the November cold and with slickers around their shoulders to combat the constant drizzle. In defeat, the early winter weather of the Cumberland Plateau along the Georgia-Tennessee state line seemed worse than it probably was.

As they broke night camp shortly after dawn some twenty hours following their departure from the lakeside on Lookout Mountain, the men heard the muted sounds of yet another battle in the distant west. And each of them according to his lights chose either to hope the Army of Tennessee was hitting back hard at the Union or to assume grimly that the Army of the Cumberland was continuing to drive the Rebels ever away from the Chattanooga area.

It was to be two days before they learned the pessimists had been right. When a war correspondent, replaced by another reporter and heading back to his newspaper in Charleston, shared a meal with D Troop and told how the Union had taken Missionary Ridge. In a spontaneous hell-for-leather assault that was not ordered by any officer; the men simply taking it into their heads to race up the ridge as fast as the steep terrain would allow. Yelling, cursing and blasting a hail of rifle and revolver fire at the Rebels. In an attack that their watching officers feared might be suicidal. But which destiny ordained should put the Confederates into full retreat and result in the Rebel victory of Chickamauga a month earlier being completely futile.

A greater gloom than ever accompanied the troop throughout the afternoon as the men pondered what the newspaper reporter had told them. And during that night as they camped in a ravine, the three troopers assigned to take the second spell of sentry duty deserted. The veteran trooper – a sergeant in the south-west territories who was reduced to the ranks before the war – who woke Steele to report that the men were missing, asked: 'How many you goin' to send after them yellow bellies, Lieutenant?'

'Nobody, trooper,' the Virginian told him wearily.

'But that's crazy, sir. If they ain't caught and shot, no tellin' how many other men are goin' to take off.'

Steele looked around at the troopers, some still asleep and others roused by the veteran when he woke their commanding officer. 'You've got a point, Barstow,' he allowed. 'But if any more men have lost the stomach for fighting, rather they did something about it at a time like now. Better than have them desert when the going gets tough. Because when that happens, I want to be sure I can count on every man in the troop.'

47

'You're the boss, sir,' the grizzle-faced Barstow acknowledged grimly. 'Guess I can only hope I bump into them three some other time. In or out of the damn war.'

Steele lay down again and drew his blankets up to his chin. 'If that's to be, feller,' he growled softly, 'it'll be a question of which of us sees them first.'

The rain let up during that night, the fourth they had spent encamped in the rugged mountains of north-western Georgia. And although the weather was bitterly cold the next morning, a watery sun hung low in the sky and visibility was good. The brightness of the day acted to hearten the men a little and they rode more erect in their saddles: did not gripe so much when the steepness of the terrain forced them to the ground to lead their horses. The occasional wisecrack drew some laughter.

Then, at mid-morning, Sergeant Grady who was riding as forward scout galloped his horse back to the troop to report that he had spotted their initial objective – the tracks of the Western and Atlantic Railroad which cut a diagonal line from close to Chattanooga all the way to central Georgia.

This sighting by one of his men was enough for Steele to halt and dismount the troopers so that he could read and study the sealed orders which had come to him via Tyson from General Braxton Bragg. And he sat on a flat rock to do this, apart from the men who smoked, re-read ancient letters from loved ones, talked or watched anxiously for a reaction from their officer.

Inside the envelope there was just a single sheet of paper with the orders taking up less than three-quarters of its space. Written in a neat script that bore no relationship to the scrawled signature of Bragg, the orders were as clear as they were concise.

My dear Captain Tyson:
From a reliable source of intelligence it would seem that

48

the Union forces in this area are now strong enough and sufficiently well supplied to mount a major offensive before this harsh winter sets in. Although the Army of Tennessee will attempt every feasible strategy to block the way into Georgia we must give as much consideration to failure as to success.

Your assignment, captain, assumes the former. In which eventuality, the railroad where you are now situated will provide the Union with an excellent route over which to bring men and supplies deep into the heartland of Georgia.

Your orders, therefore, are to do whatever is possible to hinder the Union in making use of this line of communication.

I hope and will constantly pray that you and your men survive in your efforts to slow the advance. But I fear there will be casualties. Which you will find easier to bear by knowing that every small delay you inflict upon the enemy will improve the chances of success when the Confederacy mounts a counter-offensive in the spring of 1884.

If events go according to plan here, these orders may be ignored and you are countermanded to report with your men back to your corps. If they do not, I wish you luck in your endeavours. May God go with all of you.

Braxton Bragg, General CSA.

While Steele was reading the letter addressed to a dead officer he was aware of a gradual hush that settled over the group of troopers. But not until he looked up and saw they were all watching him with lively interest was he conscious of the involuntary smile that had spread across his face.

'You look like you've just read the war's gonna be over before Christmas, sir,' a trooper named Levy said brightly, obviously half-hopeful he was somewhere near the truth.

Steele got to his feet and gave a slight nod. 'Reckon you could say the war as most of us have known it is already over,' he answered and thrust the orders toward Grady. 'Here, sergeant, read this to the men.'

While the non-com did this, the Virginian studied the faces of the troopers. And saw that Grady himself, Barstow and three others were as happy with the orders as he was. Five were indifferent – as indifferent as only battle-weary soldiers can be in response to some new orders which might lead them to being killed. Two were afraid.

'Hell, sir,' the very Jewish-featured Levy said morosely. 'This means that if our boys pulled back from south of Chattanooga, we gotta fight the whole Union army on our own. With no one to back us up if things go wrong.'

'That's right, trooper,' Steele agreed. 'Which means we're a cavalry troop doing what the cavalry do best in this kind of war. Hitting and running, just like Jeb Stuart always wanted to do. And the way Nathan Forrest does.'

'Them top brass officers got a few more men than you have, lieutenant,' another anxious trooper, named Clayburn, complained.

Enthusiasm for the assignment was a warm glow inside Adam Steele and it almost got the better of him: was on the point of advancing the debate with the men on the pros and cons of the orders. But he checked the impulse in time. And forced his face to assume an impassive expression as he took the letter back from Grady and snapped: 'We have what we have and we know what we have to do!'

He went to his horse and swung up into the saddle. 'Get mounted and follow me. Any man has a constructive suggestion to make at any time, I'll listen to him. You have complaints, save them for the next chance you have to write home.'

This said, he heeled his horse forward before all the troopers were mounted: eager to reach the railroad and

50

thereafter to make use of the free rein which had been handed him. To do what he considered would cause most harm to the enemy without need to refer to higher authority.

Hell, he thought with a grin as he demanded a gallop from the gelding, he now had more freedom than when he was managing the plantation. Where there were the ever-present watching eyes and steadying influence of his father to hamper his initiative.

He galloped across the face of a gentle slope and slowed the pace to enter a thick stand of timber at the point where he had seen Sergeant Grady emerge. Then reined in his mount at the far fringe of the trees, on the brow of a hill from which he could look down into a rocky valley through which the tracks of the railroad ran. Just for a moment the wheel-polished metals glinted in the wintery sunlight. Then grey clouds, harbingers of more bad weather, stole the brightness from the day. And Lieutenant Adam Steele, hearing the thirteen men of his troop riding through the timber behind him, felt the enthusiasm drain out of him.

He had got what he wanted – yearned for from the moment he had become disenchanted with the way so many of his superior officers, from mere captains to General Robert E Lee himself, waged war. But during times of quiet reflection upon his attitude toward authority, he was always willing to admit its basis was the human instinct that made most men resentful of taking orders.

In the past he had had to deal with this resentment from the troopers he commanded and apart from one notable failure when he lost an entire troop and the ammunition wagons they were escorting, he had succeeded. But this had always been against a background of the omnipotent – and omnipresent – army chain of command. In situations – even assignments which took them far beyond the immediate reach of high authority – where men who might contemplate rebellion against a mere volunteer wartime lieutenant, were held in check by being conscious of that all-powerful command chain that stretched out above him.

This was the army way: an established restriction against indiscipline that had been tried and tested since the first two armies were raised to fight each other.

The men reached the point where Steele sat astride the gelding, and moved their own horses out in a line so they could all look down into the valley through which the railroad ran. Men like Levy and Clayburn who were already uneasy to be outside the army establishment, missing the sense of security they drew from it. And others like Barlow and like Sergeant Grady. Barlow had already questioned one of Steele's decisions – not to seek out the trio of deserters. Had that been an impulsive reaction by the trooper: or was it a first, calculated testing of a young war officer by a soured veteran career soldier? Grady had not put a foot wrong in showing that he was aware of his responsibilities as a sergeant. And a couple of troopers had displayed traits which might mean they were fit to command. For how long would these men follow orders if they did not agree with them? At what point would they become as disenchanted with Steele as was he with his superiors?

'What now, lieutenant?' Barlow growled through his hands which were clenched to his mouth so that he could blow warm breath into the palms. 'I'd say that sky is fixin' to snow on us pretty soon.'

The Virginian had spent just a few moments contemplating the problems he might have in maintaining discipline among the troop. Then, without coming to any concrete conclusion on a point that was purely academic, he had raked his gaze along the length of the valley beneath the threatening, slate-grey sky.

'The Yankees are up north, so that's the way we go,

trooper,' Steele answered evenly. 'As far as we need to find shelter. Unless the snow hits us first. In which case we'll have to take whatever we can get.'

'Snow or the Yankees,' the young, blond-haired Clayburn said morosely, his breath misting and a shudder running through his lanky frame.

Steele fixed the young trooper with a hard gaze as he warned: 'It's going to be a long, cold winter, trooper. So you're going to have to keep warm best way you can. And make especially sure you don't get cold feet.'

Somebody laughed, but the sound was immediately masked by the hooves of the horses on the sodden ground as the men started their mounts in the wake of Steele.

Because of the panoramic view it provided, the Virginian stayed on the top of the valley side, even though the bottom land over which the railroad track was laid offered an easier and faster route. But during the remainder of the morning and the first hour of the afternoon when the troop was halted and dismounted to eat a meal of dried beef and beans, there was nothing to be seen except the vast, empty valley which had a brooding look, shadowless beneath the low, menacing sky.

The first flakes of snow drifted lazily out of the clouds as the men cleaned their eating utensils. The prospect of riding blindly through a white storm immediately dispelled whatever sense of well-being the troop had derived from putting hot food and coffee inside them. But it was just a flurry, over in minutes, and the gloomy valley remained in clear view to the file of fourteen riders until they reached its northern end. Where the terrain was less rugged, stretching away in three directions as an expanse of rolling hills with jagged ridges marking the horizon.

Just over the crest of one of these hills, which the railroad climbed in a gentle curve, was a group of frame buildings. Certain of his position after studying a military map during the meal stop, Steele was warily surprised to see the buildings. For they were not marked on the map.

'Looks abandoned, sir,' Grady said as the troop studied the single-storey buildings over a distance of almost two miles. 'If anyone was there, they'd be sure to have a fire. Weather like this.'

Steele acknowledged the comments with a non-committal grunt as he focused a pair of field glasses on the tiny community.

There was a water tower with a small shack at the base of the trestle legs immediately alongside the railroad track. Back from this, across the end of a road that swung away to the east, was a larger building with a stone smoke stack at one wall. Separated from this by a yard, enclosed by a fence which had collapsed in many places, was what looked like a store barn.

'Water and fuel halt,' he told the men as he replaced the field glasses in a saddlebag. 'Looks not to have been used in a long time. But I reckon we can make use of it.'

'Right on,' Barlow said with a grin of relish that became a challenging look as he glanced up at the dirty coloured sky.

'Easy, trooper,' Steele growled. 'We have plenty of time. You, Levy, Osborne and Trotter come with me. We'll approach along the railroad. Sergeant, take four men and move in from the north. Four more head in a direct line from here.'

'You see somethin' through them glasses our eyes didn't, lieutenant?' a man named Tripp asked nervously, as he and many of the others stared hard at the cluster of buildings.

'The same, only it looked bigger,' the Virginian answered. 'Some frame walls that most likely have nothing on the other side of them. But what's most likely isn't always necessarily how it is.'

'Just do like you're told, trooper!' Grady snapped in a

harsher tone to the short and flabbily-built Tripp. 'Which right now is to come with me. And you, Swan, York and Peck. Reynolds, you take Clayburn, Armistead and Conner and make a beeline for the place from here. You'll start to move forward when you see that the lieutenant and his men are in position. And your move will be our signal.' He looked at Steele and received a nod of approval. 'And remember what the lieutenant said. We got plenty of time.'

The troop split into three sections and while four men remained where they were, five angled one way and five the other until the track was reached to north and south of the buildings.

All the men with a clear view of the objective watched it closely, affected by the caution which had influenced Steele from the start.

The lieutenant and his men were out of sight of the rail halt for a long time, while the hill crest to the south of it intervened. Close to the top of the rise, Levy rasped: 'If there's anyone in those buildings, sir, they got to know we're around. Must have seen us when we first spotted the place. If they didn't, the rest of the fellers are in plain enough view by now.'

'You just talking to keep yourself company, trooper?' Steele asked flatly.

'No, sir. I'm just thinking that we're going to feel real foolish if there isn't any living thing inside except for a bunch of spiders or something like that.'

They crested the hill and a horse snorted. Not one of those being ridden slowly toward the group of buildings.

'I ain't never heard no spider make a noise like that, Dave,' the ugly-featured Trotter growled, and slid his Spencer out of the boot.

Which was a match for the action of every man in each group, as all eyes raked toward the barn from which the sound had come.

'All right, all right, you found us!'

The voice, shrill with fear, came from the house.

'We're comin' out! Unarmed!' Another man, bitter rather than afraid.

The door swung open, hard and fast. And crashed against the outside wall. Two men stepped across the threshold, arms thrust high above their heads. Familiar-looking men attired in Confederate grey.

'Them yellow sonsofbitches!' Barlow snarled, threw the Spencer stock to his shoulder and exploded a shot.

'No!' Steele roared, and jerked on his reins to veer his horse to the side. Colliding his mount with that of Barlow and knocking the trooper out of his saddle and into the water tower.

But the move was too late to spoil the shot, which drove a bullet into the chest of one of the men in the doorway.

'I told you, I told you!' a man screamed from inside the house. And started to open fire with a revolver before he lunged out through the doorway, leaping over the corpse of the man Barlow had killed.

The first group of troopers he saw was comprised of Reynolds, Clayburn, Armistead and Conner. Who had halted their mounts on the railroad just beyond the shack under the water tower. And it was at these men that he emptied his gun as he staggered to the centre of the trail's end. Dropping Clayburn and Conner before he was stopped by a murderous crossfire from either side of him as both Steele's group and that led by Grady exploded bullets into him. He was turned one way and then the other by the impact of the lead striking his flesh. Then he dropped to his knees and pitched forward, with still more wounds spraying blood after he was dead but the momentum of his fall had not ended.

'You murderin' mother-fu . . . ' the third man started to shriek as he brought his arms down to his sides, made to

56

turn and re-enter the house.

Instinctively, gun barrels were swung to cover him.

'Hold still, trooper!' Steele roared. And could never know if he was right in his feeling that the man, who had curtailed the obscenity, was an instant short of freezing into immobility. For another volley of shots, so close together that they made just a single report, drove bullets into his back, his side and his head. With sufficient force to lift his booted feet clear of the ground and toss him bodily in through the doorway.

There then followed stretched seconds of silence, broken when the horse in the barn snorted once again.

Barlow complained: 'You didn't have to knock me off my damn horse, sir.'

Clayburn wailed: 'If I don't get help, I'm gonna bleed to death.'

And the rest of the troop with the exception of the sprawled-face-down Conners, gazed in apprehensive silence at Steele. Who, with slow deliberation, feeling his way with gloved hands while he stared fixedly down at Barlow, extracted the spent shellcase from the Spencer and pushed a fresh round into the breech.

The veteran busted sergeant was still groggy from the fall and did not become aware of the Virginian's cold-eyed survey until he was on his feet and leaning against a water tower support. When he swallowed hard and wiped the back of a hand across his mouth. Had difficulty in tearing his eyes away from the trapping stare of Steele.

'Can you give me one good reason, trooper,' the lieutenant asked evenly as he drew a bead on Barlow's chest, 'why I shouldn't shoot you dead where you stand?'

The man swallowed hard again. Then blurted: 'Sir, them three were the men that deserted. They deserved everythin' they got!'

'Sir, please help me?' Clayburn begged, clawing with

both hands at his right thigh where a wound was pumping bright crimson blood between his fingers.

'See what can be done, sergeant,' the Virginian ordered without shifting his gaze from the grizzled face of Barlow. 'Not a good enough reason, feller. To spare a man who did what you did.'

'But they were deserters!' Barlow repeated hoarsely.

'I don't care if all three of them were the devil incarnate!' Steele snarled, his voice and expression indicating the depth of his anger for the first time. 'They were surrendering!'

'Lieutenant, the first two could've been settin' us up for the man inside!' Reynold called.

Steele merely grimaced in response to this suggestion. Then drew a sigh of relieved tension from several throats when he slid the reloaded carbine back in the boot and told Barlow: 'Your reason's invalid, trooper. So mine will have to serve. I didn't shoot you down like you deserved because I can't spare to lose you. First assignment, bury the three dead.'

'Four, sir,' Armistead corrected from where he squatted beside the inert Conners. 'Larry took two shots clean through the heart.'

Steele swung down from his horse and gave the disgruntled Barlow a final scowling glance. 'You heard the man, trooper. Get to work. And when you're down real deep and using every curse you know, remember, it's a hole you got yourself into.'

CHAPTER FOUR

IF the deserters had not been gunned down there was a good chance they would have frozen to death in a short time. Because in their haste to leave D Troop's night camp they had neglected to take matches with them. Or if they had, they had lost them or maybe expended them wastefully.

There would be no other explanation for why they had spent at least a night and the best part of a day in the abandoned house of a railroad company man without making use of the serviceable stove and ample supplies of kindling and cordwood for a fire to warm themselves and heat their food.

Unless they were afraid that the smoke from such a fire would attract unwelcome attention.

But yet again, Adam Steele wasted little time in pondering a question the answer to which could never be known and, anyway, was irrelevant.

What was important was that the troop and their mounts had adequate shelter from the snow storm that hit the hill country within two hours of the horses being bedded down in the barn. And an hour later the men were eating a hot meal in the warmth and relative comfort of the spartanly furnished house. With no need for sentries to be posted outside, in weather that veiled everything more than a few inches away in an impenetrable curtain of pure white.

The house was not much. Just two rooms – a combination parlour and kitchen with a small bedroom formed by matchboard partitions in one corner. Clayburn, his flesh-wounded thigh bound, lay in the bedroom on his blankets on the floor. Weak from loss of blood, and sleeping. In the main room there was a table and two chairs with the backs missing, and the stove. Steele claimed the table and one of the chairs to turn a corner of the room into a makeshift office. While the men ate on the floor, seated on their saddles, and afterwards spread their bedrolls wherever it suited them. Light was provided by candles and a glow from the stove.

Before the fire was lit with kindling and fuel which was heaped in a corner of the barn, the place had smelled dank with damp and decay. But with the stove roaring and the cracks around the ill-fitting door and glassless, boarded-up windows filled with wadding, the atmosphere was good to breathe. Less so for Steele and other men who did not smoke when, after the meal was over, cigarettes, cheroots and two pipes were lit and a layer of blue smoke drifted in the warm air.

At the table in the corner, the Virginian studied for awhile those military maps which had a bearing on the assignment. And, as he listened to the whine of the wind around the buildings of the railroad fuel halt, his enthusiasm for Braxton Bragg's plan faltered. But did not die.

In terms of major engagements, the war was going to grind to a halt for the winter: for much as the Union would desire to push southwards and take advantage of their recent victories, the weather was against such an advance. Which meant that until the spring, when fine weather would allow for the mass movement of men, heavy armaments and supplies, D Troop was to operate in a vast empty area of no-man's-land between the two resting armies. Operating as a seek and destroy unit, but with precious few objectives that were a feasible proposition for such a small troop.

'Somethin' botherin' you, lieutenant?' Grady asked as he signalled a request to sit on the second backless chair at the side of the table.

Steele gave tacit assent, then realised how weary he was as he glanced around the crowded room and saw that every other trooper was asleep on his bedroll.

'Small matter of how and where to find the enemy, feller,' the Virginian answered flatly.

In repose, the thin face of the tall and rangily built non-com had a naturally sorrowful expression – as if he was constantly reflecting on a piece of bad news. 'All due respect, sir,' he said. 'It ain't just me who holds the opinion that General Bragg ain't all he's cracked up to be.'

Steele showed a quiet grin that served to drop away from his face the ageing lines which war had carved into the flesh. 'I can't criticise him for the orders. He's not the only one to whom it seemed like a good idea at the time.'

Grady, who at thirty was four years the Virginian's senior, expressed a smile of his own: which went only part way to dispelling the aura of melancholy that clung to the man. 'I'm no great thinker, sir. Always got by knowin' what I know and pickin' up more as I went along. Before the war, I hunted and fished country like this. But never this time of year. When I read them orders to the men, figured then we had more chance dyin' from the cold as with a Yankee bullet in us. Unless the bluebellies had the same hairbrained scheme to send men out into country at a time when even the animals have the sense to go to sleep until the cold's over.'

Steele nodded in ackowledgement of the sergeant's assessment of the situation. 'Go along with you all the way, feller. But because I outrank you and here and now there's nobody around to outrank me, I have to take it further. And I have.'

'Sir?'

'You hit it when you spoke of animals hibernating for the winter. Which is what we're going to do, in a manner of speaking.'

'Sir?' Grady said again. But it was not simply a bald query this time. He was also questioning the soundness of the Virginian's reasoning.

'We have shelter from the elements, ample fuel to keep us warm, an unlimited supply of water and at least two experienced hunters – you and me – to keep us fed off those animals that do not hiberate.'

Grady pondered the points for long moments. Then showed another melancholic smile. 'It sounds good, lieutenant,' he allowed at length.

'But it doesn't end there,' Steele went on. 'We've reached the place where the orders said we should be. Dead centre of the line of advance the Union will take. In time. Time for us to familiarise ourselves with the terrain and find those locations where we'll best be able to carry out the main purpose of Bragg's orders. Whenever the weather allows.'

'Got you, sir,' Grady rasped with enthusiasm.

'That's good,' Steele replied grimly. 'Make sure the men see it your way. And make sure, too, that they know they're going to have to work their butts off to stay alive through the winter and have a better than even chance of surviving the Union advance when it comes. I want this place run on the same lines as a regular army post, sergeant. There'll be drills, inspections, officer's reports, post policing and recreational periods. I'm promoting Troopers Reynolds and York to the rank of corporal to give you a hand in seeing the daily routine is maintained.'

This daily routine took several days to become an established pattern. Days of experimentation and sour-voiced complaints about snot-nosed young officers who got too big for their boots and never knew when to let up on hard driving of the men under their command. But eventually the post by the railroad in the snow-covered wilderness – which was unofficially christened Camp Crazy – began to run smoothly.

That first night in the railroadman's shack when Steele had formulated his plan for the winter, he had been doubtful about just one factor – the inevitable boredom that was always a part of army life at an isolated camp when the duty period was over. But in the event this proved not to be a problem. For after long hours in the biting cold, hunting game, reducing the unwanted buildings to stove fuel, clearing snow off the pastureland so that the horses could graze and scouting the country far and wide in addition to the more normal post duties, the troopers were barely able to remain awake to eat before dropping on to their bedrolls and falling into the deep, luxurious sleep of exhaustion.

Clayburn recovered from his leg wound: and, after nursing his resentment toward Steele to no avail, Barlow integrated himself once again into the troop.

December and January came and went and Christmas and the New Year of 1864 were ignored in the same way as Thanksgiving had been.

In mid-February, a new element of warfare was introduced when a Rebel submarine sank a Yankee warship off Charleston. And a few days later, further away from Camp Crazy, the Union suffered a defeat at Olustee, Florida. Then, in March, fighting flared up in Louisiana when the Union launched its Red River Campaign to take the state. It was to last two months and prove that gunboats were useless on waterways, which in the morning allowed the craft passage and by afternoon left them grounded in the shallows.

Of course, the men of D Troop knew nothing of the progress of the war. And few of them probably would have cared about the news had it been available to them. But Steele would have been interested to learn of a Rebel victory on 12 April, when the men in grey recaptured Fort Pillow, Tennessee. For it was to this stronghold on the Mississippi River that he had been bound in the early June of 1862 when a women-inspired mutiny by his troop had led to the loss of a desperately needed wagon train of ammunition.

At the end of that same April, D Troop saw their first action of the year. The snow was long gone, washed away by heavy rain rather than melted by the sun on the few bright days that came to the Cumberland Plateau during the spring.

The first indication the men received that they were about to become involved in a shooting war again was a sighting of black smoke above a distant hill in the north. It was a cloudy morning, with the sky low and grey and threatening more rain – which held off for long enough so that Steele was able to plot the smoke on a map and decide it was being expelled by a slow-moving locomotive.

'Okay, sergeant, we're moving out,' the Virginian announced as the first spots of rain fell, staining the map before he was able to fold it and push it into his belt pouch. 'The timber on the north hill.'

'To the horses and mount up!' Grady yelled. 'Let's get this war finished so we can all go home!'

There was eagerness in his voice and in the words and actions of the men as they made haste to comply with the order.

'We goin' for good, lieutenant?' the no-longer flabby Tripp asked, the excess flesh at his belly and chest having been shed as part of the toughening process which had affected all the men during the harsh winter.

'Got to feel a little like some kind of home to you, too, trooper?' Steele countered.

'The best kind I ever did have, sir,' Tripp answered with a final glance at the shack before he followed the others toward the barn.

Then, within ten minutes, the railroad fuel and water halt was as deserted as it had been before the trio of deserters from D Troop entered it. But it presented a different sight to that which they and then the rest of the cavalrymen had first looked upon. For the water tower and the shack beneath it, the fence which had enclosed the yard, and a large part of the barn cum a stable had been torn down and broken up to feed the fire which had burned so long in the stove.

But to anybody seeing it now for the first time, there was nothing to indicate that what remained had served as winter quarters for thirteen men. For spring growth had taken over the sites of the destroyed structures. And within minutes of the horses carrying their riders out of the immediate vicinity, the teeming rain filled the hoofprints which were soon disguised as the sides of the impressions caved in.

In the timber on the brow of a hill a half mile due north of Camp Crazy, Steele ordered the men to dismount, keep their horses quiet and keep watch: with loaded carbines in their hands.

The two remaining buildings beneath the brow of the next hill south were blurred by the rain, but the troopers had a clear view of the railroad where it curved around the base of their vantage point. And of the ten Union cavalrymen who rode into sight at the side of the track.

The downward range was less than two hundred yards and Steele could sense the tension of excitement which gripped his men as they saw the enemy for the first time in many months.

'Any man opens fire unless ordered to do so faces a field court-martial, sergeant, Steele rasped. 'Pass it on.'

Grady did so, stepping carefully among the dripping brush under the trees to whisper the warning to each man in turn. Then, by the time he returned to the lieutenant's side, the casually riding, easy talking Yankee troopers were out of earshot. Heading up the side of the south hill toward the buildings. And the sounds of the straining locomotive and a string of clattering cars could be heard by the Rebels: first against the hiss of the rain and then masking it.

Moments later the train rolled into sight. There were, in fact, two Camelback locomotives, hauling a long line of flatbed freight cars with what they carried protected from the weather by tightly lashed down sheets of burlap. In addition to the crews, two soldiers rode on each footplate. And, Steele reckoned, it was a safe bet that there was also a military presence aboard the caboose.

'Been better if she was rollin' faster, sir,' Grady rasped as the rain-laced air became tainted with the acrid smoke from the locomotives' stacks.

'Everythin is what only the luckiest folks have,' Steele answered as, like every man at the edge of the timber, he fixed his expectant gaze upon the point at which the track began the up-grade toward the buildings.

'And we're thirteen,' Barlow muttered. Vented an almost girlish giggle of pleasure and added: 'Which is real unlucky for them bluebellies.'

The rails immediately ahead of the leading locomotive began to buckle and there was a great billow of steam from beneath it as the engineer realised something was wrong and fought to halt the train. But the ten mile an hour momentum did not give him the time.

The ground opened up, the front of the locomotive dipped and the rails ahead snapped like matchsticks and sprang skywards.

The coupling between the rear of the first engine and the front of the second one sheered.

The front engine slid down into the fifteen-foot-deep pit and veered to the right before rolling on to its side.

The second Camelback tilted and smashed into the underneath of the first.

At least one tank of scalding water burst and exploded billowing steam into the air.

This as the line of freight cars came to a sudden, shuddering halt, only the first one leaving the rails.

'Hot damn, we did it!' the unchevroned Corporal Reynolds exclaimed, the joy in his voice expressing what every man in D Troop felt as he witnessed the train wreck which had taken so many muscle-aching, sweating, cursing hours to bring about.

First in the digging out of the pit. Then in the scattering far and wide of the displaced earth. Next the shoring up with timber of boards on which the track bed could be relaid in such a manner that a locomotive crew would be unaware of the trap until it was too late.

Now two men scrambled up out of the pit in which the two crippled locomotives lay. One of them in uniform and screaming as he held both hands over his face. The second in oil-stained coveralls.

This as half a dozen uniformed men leapt down from the caboose and the horsemen – who had almost reached the buildings at the time of the wreck – came racing back down the hill.

All the soldiers except for the man with an injured face had carbines or revolvers in their hands, as their frightened eyes raked the rain-lashed country on all sides, seeking a sign that the wreck was just the opening round in a full-scale attack.

'Easy, easy,' Steele said evenly as his men licked their lips and took a tighter grip on their Spencers: bristling like a pack of hounds eager to be let loose for the kill.

For a full minute the hiss of steam from the crippled locomotives masked all other sounds at the railroad while the foot soldiers and cavalrymen stretched out in a thin defensive line to either side of the stalled freight cars. Then, as this was subdued, the voice of the crewman kneeling beside the now prostrated wounded soldier could be heard.

'Somebody help here! This guy's had the skin scalded off his face! And maybe there's some others alive in the friggin' hole!'

Orders were yelled and acknowledged.

Ten blue-clad men climbed up on top of the freight cars to continue to watch for attackers while the other six ran to the head of the train. One to comfort his scalded comrade while the rest clambered down into the pit to check for survivors.

Time elapsed.

The men atop the cars became less concerned with the apparently empty terrain and cast frequent glances to where inert forms were being brought up from the pair of now almost silent locomotives.

While in the timber, exhilaration abated and scowls and frowns spread on the faces of the Rebel troopers. Some were resentful of being held back in hiding at a time when they were keyed up and ready to finish off the job while the adrenalin was running. To others, this period of waiting allowed them time to reflect on dying at the hands of the Yankees on and beside the train – something there would have been no opportunity to do had Steele ordered them into an attack when excitement still gripped them.

But still the Virginian gave no command: waited until the men below had counted their dead and relaxed their vigilance as they investigated the cause of the wreck.

'What was it, captain?' a private asked. 'Weather

undermine the track?'

'Mount up,' Steele said and swung into his own saddle.

'No friggin' way, soldier boy!' the sole survivor of the train crews snarled. 'I seen washed out track before and they was never like this!'

'Attend to your sentry duty!' the infantry captain snapped at the man who had posed the question. Then returned to a low-voiced conversation with the cavalry captain and lieutenant at the side of the pit.

Steele spoke low and fast to Grady while the men were getting mounted and now the sergeant pointed to six troopers in turn and signalled that they should form up behind him. The Virginian signalled the remaining five to join him. Then the officer and the non-com each outlined the plan of attack to his platoon and, grim-faced, every man fixed a bayonet to his carbine.

'Ready?' Steele asked.

He and Grady raked their eyes over the face of each individual and received a nod.

'Go!'

Heels thudded into flanks and voices were raised. In encouragement for the horses to give maximum speed. Or to vent the Rebel yell for the ears of the startled Yankees.

The troopers burst from the timber in two distinct groups astride their mounts. Grady and his men riding for the centre of the line of cars while Steele led his men toward the wrecked engines in the pit.

Panic gripped many of the Union soldiers and several carbines were exploded instinctively in the direction of the charging Rebel cavalry: the discharged bullets going hopelessly wild.

'Let them have it, boys!' Grady roared as he and his men triggered a volley of carbine fire at the Yankee atop the freight cars.

'Fire at will!' Steele shouted in a more orthodox

expression of the order. Which drew a similar response from the men he led.

Because the Rebels were astride horses riding downhill at a full-tilt gallop through the lancing rain, the bullets which left the gun barrels were less than carefully placed. The men having to fire the Spencers one-handed while the other was busy with the reins.

The locomotive engineer was sent staggering into the pit with a bloody stain showing at the crotch of his coveralls. And two of the soldiers making haste to get down from the cars were pitched into involuntary falls by bullets tunnelling through their flesh.

But these were lucky hits for the Confederate cavalry: this opening fusillade of shots intended simply to provide cover for the charge, while the Union men scrambled for safety behind the wrecked locomotives and the stalled line of cars.

The Rebels were more than halfway to their objective by then. And much closer before the rattle of firing handguns sounded against the thunder of galloping hooves. The spray of bullets cracking toward the two groups of riders just as, according to the attack plan, they veered further apart. Steele and his men maintaining a course on the front of the train while Grady's group swung wider to close with the rear.

Steele heard a man behind him scream, then glimpsed a horse as it drew level with his own. He spared perhaps a complete second to glance away from the train. And felt an anger colder than the worst of the winter weather he had experienced take a grip on the pit of his stomach. For it was Tripp, the once fat kid who had been pared down and toughened up during his enforced stay in the best home he had ever had, who was desperately trying to stay in the saddle by clinging tightly to the neck of his mount. Face turned toward the Virginian and displaying an expression which pleaded for help as arterial blood gushed from a wound in his throat. Then, at the end of the second, another fountain of bright crimson sprang from his mouth, he lost his grip on the horse and tumbled to the sopping wet ground.

Another volley of revolver fire cracked out. Closely followed by the louder reports of a few carbines, these shots exploded by Yankees who had taken the time to reload.

The riderless horse stumbled and fell as he made to veer away from the group.

Steele, the high emotion of his cold anger erupting sweat beads which coursed down his face with the raindrops, led his men into a tight turn around the wreckage in the pit: the horses leaping without command over the track and its bed.

Carbines with fixed bayonets were hurled like lances at the blue-clad figures who rose and turned from cover, surprised by the sudden change of direction by the Rebels.

Only two struck home, one Yankee taking two inches of metal in his heart while the second screamed to the limit of his vocal chords as the bayonet entered his belly and then showed its blood-sheened point at the small of his back.

'Hey, the bluebellies are red inside!' Levy yelled in high excitement at striking the vicious blow.

This as he and the other riders drew their revolvers: exploded shots down into the pit as they brought their horses to rearing, snorting halts.

'Enough, enough!' a voice screamed from between the two wrecked locomotives. And a hand was seen, moving violently from side to side to wave a sodden piece of rag in surrender.

'Like hell!' another of the Yankees snarled and blasted a shot at the now-halted group of Rebels.

Trooper Armistead took the bullet in the right cheek and was dead before he toppled from his saddle, an arc of blood spraying from the exit wound at the crown of his head.

'Finish them!' Steele snarled. And was the first to begin

emptying his revolver into the pit. This as he leapt out of the saddle, the better to move around the sides of the hole and locate blue-uniformed targets among the cover of the crippled locomotives.

Levy, Clayburn and Osborne followed his example, gripped so completely by the urge to avenge the death of Armistead that they ignored the danger of their own ricochets as many of their bullets cracked against the metal of the locomotives and spun off on a different trajectory.

'Lieutenant!' somebody called. Then bellowed again: 'Lieutenant!'

Steele and the three troopers had emptied their handguns, but the Virginian still felt an urgent need to find a fresh outlet for the ice-cold rage that seemed to bloat his stomach. And he leapt on to the tank of the overturned locomotive. Vaguely aware that all shooting had now ended as he thrust the Dance Brothers revolver back into his holster. Then reached down to draw the knife from the sheath strapped to his right calf.

'Lieutenant, we got to get outta here!' Sergeant Grady roared.

Steele's gloved right hand emerged from the split in the side of his pants leg and the nine other Rebels who had survived the attack stared in fascination at their officer. They knew about the concealed weapon – had often seen him draw and use the knife during the winter months: to clean and gut a dead animal or fashion a piece of lumber into a necessary tool. But never had they witnessed it plunging into flesh. As it did now.

The Union cavalry captain was already wounded, blood blossoming around a bullet hole in his right shoulder. Like Steele, he had no firearm. At first seemed to be without a weapon of any kind. Until he raised his left hand to his yellow kerchief. And drew from it a pearl-headed stickpin. Which he clutched in his fist with a full two inches of its length protruding viciously from the heel of his hand.

The tall, slim, handsome Yankee officer spared a scornful look at the troopers beside the pit as he rose from cover. And then fixed Steele with a stare of greater contempt as he rasped: 'I don't expect a fair fight with yellow Rebels.'

From the north came the sound of a bugle blast. It was the first time Steele had heard this signal that Union reinforcements were on their way. Not so Grady: 'I been tryin' to tell you, sir, we ought . . . '

The Union captain was hauling himself up on to the tank of the locomotive, hampered by the painful wound in his shoulder.

Steele's booted feet rang against the metal. Then one of them was lowered on to the wrist of the hand fisted around the stickpin. And the man became rigid, fresh pain contorting his handsome features as he twisted his head to look up at the Virginian.

'We don't always get what we expect, captain,' Steele said coldly as he stooped. 'War's like love. All's fair.'

He used the flat of the knife blade to tilt the man's head up even more. Then thrust it hard and fast downwards: burying it into the Yankee's throat before the point was obstructed by the top of his spine.

'You're all right, lieutenant,' somebody said. Steele thought it was probably the veteran Barlow.

He waited until the death spasm had ceased to move his victim, then withdrew the knife and held it out to the side for the rain to wash off the blood as he claimed the stickpin and pushed it into the collar of his tunic.

'Sir?' Grady said anxiously as the bugle call sounded again. Much closer than before.

'Every Yankee dead?' Steele asked and straightened after replacing the knife in the sheath.

'Yes, sir,' the non-com responded.

Steele nodded and felt the tension of rage and anger drain

out of him as his face altered its lines to show an expression of impassivity. This as he leapt off the overturned locomotive on to the soft ground beside the pit. Noting that one of Grady's men was missing.

'You've had a casualty, sergeant?'

'Trooper Swan, sir. Shot dead.'

'Then there were ten,' Barlow said lightly.

Steele retrieved his own Spencer and unfixed the bayonet which had failed to hit a target. 'Gather your weapons, reload and capture any loose horses you can find in two minutes.'

While the men complied with the order, Steele drew the knife again and cut through two ropes so that he was able to lift a corner of the burlap sheeting covering the freight on the first car. The cargo was wooden cases of rations.

'Ready, sir,' Grady reported as Steele finished reloading his Dance Brothers revolver beside the partially uncovered freight car. 'Lucky it wasn't ammunition, lieutenant. Or we could all have been blown to kingdom come, the way so much lead was flyin' around.'

'There's food for thought, sergeant,' the Virginian allowed grimly as he swung up astride his own horse and slid the carbine in the boot.

'Tell you somethin', lieutenant,' Levy growled as the bugler to the north sounded another blast.

'Move out!' Steele commanded and heeled his horse forward.

'Don't know what kinda grub is aboard that train,' Levy said to the ugly Trotter riding beside him. 'But we sure made mincemeat out of the guys supposed to guard it.'

Only Levy himself laughed at his joke, and then this sound was masked by the galloping hooves of ten horses with men astride them, and seven on lead lines whose former riders were dead.

And the attackers who had wrought such havoc on the

supply train were long gone beyond the curtain of lashing rain when the column of Union cavalrymen galloped around the base of the hill to the north and discovered the wreckage and the dead men.

CHAPTER FIVE

THE Union cavalry did not set out in pursuit of the Rebel troopers, for they and the supply train which had preceded them were part of a Northern scheme of things which had far bigger fish to fry. And in the overall progress of the Yankee offensive against the Confederacy in that spring of 1864, D Troop's assault on the train was little more than mild irritation to General William T Sherman who masterminded the advance on Atlanta.

But in the minds of Lieutenant Adam Steele and the troopers the one-sided battle at the railroad north of Camp Crazy was firmly lodged as a triumphant success in terms of the kind of war they had been ordered to fight.

And as they withdrew to a cave in the broad valley where they had first reached the railroad, from which they emerged to tear up sections of track and monitor the massing of the Union army, the winter-hardened men in grey felt fully satisfied with the outcome of their initial blow against the enemy.

The rain continued to pour from out of the miserable grey sky and the temperature in the hills remained low. But although the weather meant the troopers were constantly cold and wet, it did provided them with cover while they watched the Union build up and carried out their destructive delaying tactics.

Inside the cave conditions shared by men and animals were reasonably good – except when compared with the relative luxury of Camp Crazy. But the men merely slept or ate cold meals in here: for the greater part of the time they were outside in the rain on foot. Engaged with duties which quickly palled as they recalled the exhilaration of the train wreck and the battle that followed it.

For three days D Troop maintained this routine, many of the men becoming frustrated and restless at being within easy range of the enemy but with orders not to open fire unless they were spotted. While Steele's discontent arose from another source – the fact that there was not a sign of the Confederacy moving up men to meet the Union forces.

Then, minus the spare horses but with the contents of their saddlebags transferred, the ten men left the cave at nightfall and rode in slow single file southwards along the top of the valley side: constantly looking over their shoulders for Union skirmishers or peering intently ahead for Confederates who might open fire in the darkness and rain without demanding to know who they were shooting at. But they neither saw nor heard anything.

Until, as the first light of grey dawn relieved the dark of night, their vigilance was rewarded. When, as Steele and Grady made to lead the men around a thick stand of timber, a voice was heard.

'Okay, you men. Up and on your horses. Time to move out.'

Every Rebel cavalryman heard the gruffly spoken words and there was no need for either the Virginian or the non-com to signal the order. The slow-moving horses were reined to a halt and hands reached forward to keep the animals from making any sound.

Steele and Grady slid from their saddles and eased the carbines from the boots before handing their reins to Osborne and York. Then went forward on foot for a few yards, staying close to the dripping trees. Reached a point from which they could peer between two pine trunks at a group of six men: one already in the process of saddling his horse while the others wearily rose from their bedrolls and began to furl them.

Although the light was murky beneath the trees on the fringe of the timber stand and the group was breaking camp a hundred yards away, it was possible to see that the men were attired in civilian garb. Some of them were talking, but in tones too low for what they were saying to make any sense to the two watching Rebel troopers.

Steele held his Spencer in the crook of an arm and held up eight fingers in front of Grady. Then made a gesture with his hand to indicate that he wanted the entire troop aligned, on foot at right-angles to the edge of the timber. Continued to peer between the trunks at the men while the sergeant backed away to comply with the command. And strained his ears to pick up any stray word that might provide a clue to the identity of the six strangers.

But whenever he did catch a disjointed word or phrase it was either a curse or related to the early start and the foul weather.

All the horses were saddled and two of the men were astride their mounts when the troopers were in the formation Steele had commanded.

Steele signalled an advance and set the example of nestling the stock of the carbine to his shoulder. Waited until the squelching of the troopers' feet in the sodden grass alerted the civilian-attired men to danger before he snapped: 'Hands raised and don't move!'

There was an eighty yard gap between the two groups.

Four men were now astride horses while the other two were in the process of hauling themselves up into their saddles.

'Sonofabitch, where did they come . . . ' a man started.

'Move, they're Rebs!' another yelled.

Two of the men in the saddle thudded heels against the flanks of their horses and yelled for a gallop. While one of those not yet mounted whirled away from his horse and broke into a sprint.

'Fire!' Steele roared, and squeezed the trigger of his Spencer.

One of the riders was lifted from his saddle and thrown with a suddenly curtailed scream into a tree trunk: blood spurting from at least three bullet holes in his back and side. The other would-be escaper on horseback was also hit several times, but took longer to die as – a foot trapped in a stirrup – he was dragged off into the rainy dawn by his galloping horse.

The man on foot was brought down by a shot in the leg, then silenced and stilled by a bullet that tunnelled into his head.

One of the remaining two men in the saddle might have been as eager as the other and the one on the ground to surrender. But his horse was startled by the gunfire and, as it reared and made to turn, its hapless rider was blasted by two shots that sent him head over heels off the rump of the animal.

'For God's sake, no more!' the man on the ground shrieked, his arms reaching to their limit into the air.

The man astride the quiet horse also had his arms raised in a gesture of surrender. But he was far less emphatic and his expression was one of melancholic resignation rather than terror.

'Hold your fire!' Steele ordered as he drew his revolver and took slow paces forward.

The troopers had also drawn their handguns and matched

the Virginian's attitude and advance: revolvers cocked and levelled and carbines canted to their shoulders.

The galloping hooves of the bolted horses had now faded out of earshot and the sucking of sodden ground at booted feet sounded very loud as the soldiers moved along the fringe of the timber at the side of the meadow in the misty light of the rainy dawn.

'Seems like we had the right idea, to get away from the Rebels,' the quiet man astride the horse said dully.

He was about forty, tall and very thin with several days' growth of bristles sprouting darkly on his lower face and contrasting starkly with the paleness of his forehead and area around his sunken eyes.

'But we're gonna die anyway, Mr Grogan,' the twenty-year-old frightened man on the ground added miserably.

He was a head shorter than Grogan, but just as thin. His hair and embryonic beard were blond.

Both were dressed like farmers in old and patched denim pants and jackets with rain slickers caping their shoulders and battered hats dripping from the brims. A garb that matched that of the four men who had died. All of them, too, had revolvers protruding from the waistbands of their pants. And there were rifle stocks jutting from the makeshift boots slung from the saddles of the horses.

'We tried, Hawkins,' Grogan said. 'We did our best.'

The soldiers came to a halt, still in a line, some fifteen feet from where the two men continued to hold their arms aloft.

'Who are you?' Steele asked. 'And I already know your names.'

'Ordinary folks from around Dalton way,' Grogan answered as Hawkins turned his head to look helplessly up at him. 'Like them you and your men killed, lieutenant. Wanted no part of this war. On either side. But had our places taken over by you Rebs. One of our women raped. Managed to send our families south before anythin' worse

80

happened. Couldn't make it ourselves. In that direction. So came north.'

His voice and posture continued to express resignation to whatever was inevitable. While the younger man seemed to be having trouble trying to control the threat of an attack of trembling.

'Both of you, ease out your handguns and toss them away,' the Virginian ordered evenly. 'Then you, Grogan, get down off the horse. Any of my men even think either of you are trying something, you're both dead.'

'Do as the lieutenant tells you, boy,' Grogan said, and there was a note of authority in his voice now. Then he complied with the demand and Hawkins watched him, as if eager to have an example to follow so that he would do it right.

Both revolvers were tossed in the same direction – over to where the man had crashed off his horse into a tree before falling dead to the ground. Then the two prisoners stood side by side, arms still raised.

'Confederate army's in Dalton, you say?' Steele asked.

'Entrenched on Rocky Face Ridge north of there,' Grogan supplied. 'A little ways up from where the railroad forks out of town.'

'Grady, have some men check the corpses and the horses,' the Virginian said as he holstered the Dance Brothers revolver and slid a map from the pouch on his belt. 'Somebody else bring the horses from in back of the timber. Levy, Clayburn, keep the prisoners covered.'

While the troopers did what they were told, Steele moved into the scant shelter from the rain provided by a tree and unfolded the map to check on the mental image he had of the geography of the area. And saw he had remembered it well enough.

There was, indeed, a Rocky Face Ridge north of the town of Dalton: in the vee between two railroad tracks – one running due north and the other north-west.

The troop's present position, he judged, was perhaps fifteen miles in front of the CSA, a little east of the north-west track which came down from Chattanooga: north and east of a pass called Ringgold Gap. And if they maintained the heading they had been on since leaving the cave in the valley south of Camp Crazy, they would move directly down between the converging railroads and before nightfall would reach the area securely held by the Confederacy.

The map was only slightly dampened by drips from the tree when Steele refolded it and returned it to the pouch. The horses had been brought to the side of the meadow by then, but Grady and some of the troopers were still engaged in searching the dead and the saddlebags of those horses which had not bolted out of sight into the rain and the mist. Levy and Clayburn had moved the prisoners a little way out into the pastureland, clear of the trees and their own and the dead men's guns.

'What you gonna do with us, lieutenant?' Hawkins asked nervously, having little success in controlling his fear.

'Maybe just rob us like those other Rebels, boy,' Grogan said. 'Or maybe rob us and kill us like Sanders and King and . . . '

'What you call robbery, feller,' Steele cut in, 'in wartime is known as confiscation.' He looked hard at the older man, sensing rather than seeing any physical sign that Grogan was not as calm as he had been at first. 'And the men that were killed did not comply with my order. You two will end up that way only if I think there's a good reason for it.'

'We have surrendered our weapons and . . . '

'You may now lower your arms,' Steele allowed.

Again Hawkins waited for Grogan to give a lead. And both of them obviously welcomed the relief to their strained muscles.

'Mr Steele,' Grady said coldly as he joined the Virginian,

Levy and Clayburn in front of the prisoners, and gazed morosely at the civilian-clad men. 'I think maybe me and the boys have found a reason.'

Hawkins squeezed his eyes tightly closed and clenched his fists. Grogan swallowed hard.

'What's that, sergeant?'

'Well, sir, the whole six were carrying Remington Army revolvers and five got Starr carbines. Which is what a lot of Yankee bluebellies get issued with. And Mr Grogan here, he had some kinda foreign rifle in his boot. With a telescope sight in his saddlebag and places on the barrel where it fits. Sniper-style.'

Grogan was eager to defend himself and the others, but held back until Grady paused. 'Hell, we had those weapons before the war, lieutenant. And I used mine for huntin'. With the telescope fixed I can bring down a deer from . . . '

'Ain't all, sir,' the sergeant interrupted as the rest of the troop gathered into a group in front of hapless prisoners. 'One of the dead. Name of Sanders. Had a letter in his shirt pocket. Dated August of 1862. From his girl in Chicago. Addressed to Private Sanders, Third Army Corps, Army of Virginia in Washington.'

'Sir, we was given orders not to carry anythin' that . . . '

'Easy, private!' Grogan said flatly, but with that note of authority back in his voice. Then he came to attention and threw up a terse salute to the Virginian. 'Captain Irvin Grogan, lieutenant. On assignment from what is now designated the First Army Corps, Army of the Potomac. If you and your men had not killed Private Sanders it is likely he would have been executed for his act of disobedience. But that no longer matters. I surrender myself and Private Hawkins and request the status and privileges of prisoners of war as befits our respective ranks.'

'Up your ass, bluebelly!' Barlow rasped, and reached for his holstered revolver.

83

'Keep your mouth shut and your gun where it is, trooper!' Steele snapped, without shifting his steady gaze away from the face of the Union army captain. A face wearing an expression that belied the confidence with which Grogan had spoken. And which showed not a flicker of emotion when the Virginian responded: 'You and Hawkins are out of uniform, captain. And I don't reckon you are on furlough. Not in this part of the country. So it follows you're on active service.'

Grogan was calm again and, strangely, now that the truth was known, a great deal of the nervous tension had drained out of Hawkins.

'It was worth an attempt, lieutenant,' the older prisoner said. 'I apologise to you for even thinking I could fool you. And request that you execute Private Hawkins and myself with despatch.'

'Execute?' the ugly Trotter gasped.

'They're Union intelligence, Don,' Acting Corporal York explained absently. 'Spies who know that when they're caught, that's what happens to them.'

The new day was fully broken now and the rain was no more than a cold drizzle. Below the dome of mist that enclosed the fringe of the timber and a section of the meadow, a strange mixture of calmness and tension seemed to create an oddly bright light.

'We gonna hang them or shoot them, sir?' Barlow asked eagerly. 'Hang them is what I think we should do?'

'The lieutenant told you to hold your tongue, Barlow!' Grady snarled, obviously not relishing being involved in any kind of cold-blooded killing of the two helpless prisoners.

'Easy, sergeant,' the impassive Steele placated after a glance at the faces of every member of the troop. Which showed that only Dave Levy was as eager as the busted sergeant Barlow to apply the rule of war pertaining to captured enemy spies. For the rest of the troopers looked as uneasy as Grady. Which created the shadow of a scornful expression at the sides of Grogan's mouth. Hawkins stared straight ahead, into infinity, totally composed: and merely blinked and momentarily swept his eyes along their sockets when the Virginian approached him, halted at his side, drew the Dance Brothers revolver and thumbed back the hammer as he pressed the muzzle to the young man's left temple. 'God rest your soul,' he said coldly.

And squeezed the trigger.

The forehead of the young soldier exploded as the bullet which was angled into the temple burst into the open just above his nose. And shocked profanities were vented from the lips of several of the troopers as they heard the gunshot, saw the spray of blood and bone fragments and watched Hawkins, rigid in the moment of death, topple to the wet grass like a felled tree.

Clayburn managed to turn away and drop on all fours before his stomach erupted and the vomit splashed from his mouth.

Grady stared in abject horror at Steele.

Grogan expressed an instant of grief before he raised his eyes from the dead man to pour scorn like a physical force from his face to that of the Virginian.

'I guess that way will have to suffice, lieutenant,' he said thickly.

'It's the easy way, captain,' the Virginian answered evenly. 'Quick and, as far as anybody can know, painless.' He moved up behind the stiffly standing Union spy as he spoke, and cocked the revolver again. Smelled the sweat of fear on Grogan and heard the sharp intake of breath as he inserted the gun muzzle into the man's left armpit. 'Hard way is to see how many shots you can take and how much pain you can endure before you die.'

Still only Barlow and Levy were excited by what was happening.

Clayburn had finished throwing up and was being helped to his feet by the shocked Peck and Osborne.

'Why, lieutenant?' Grogan said, hardly moving his lips. 'Everyone here's a soldier. We do what we are told. Hawkins was issued the same orders I was.'

'And he probably knew as much as you do, captain. About the Union plans for the push into Georgia.' Although Grogan had been standing to attention for some time, there was still leeway for his back muscles to become tauter. 'But there's no sense in making two men suffer. Maybe not even one? What do you say?'

'We've been operating down south for the whole winter, lieutenant. I've got no idea what . . . '

The Dance Brothers cracked out another shot. Grogan curtailed what he was saying with a grunt of shock as he staggered half a pace forward. But then held still again, not even looking down at the blood-blossoming wound in his shoulder.

Steele moved to the same extent, and thrust the smoke-wisping muzzle into the wounded man's right armpit.

'That's it, lieutenant!' Barlow blurted with something akin to lust gleaming in his eyes.

This as Levy sucked in a deep breath and allowed it out in a long sigh.

'Shut your stinkin' mouth, trooper!' Grady ordered. But his eyes directed a portion of his deep feeling toward the Virginian.

'You were briefed before you were sent south, Captain,' Steele said with a total lack of emotion. 'And given orders where to report after you'd done your job. Hope for your sake you were given some details of how the top brass in your Union army reckoned to use the information you brought back.'

'Sir, we know where they're massin',' Grady said, fast and husky. 'And it figures they're gonna come right down the railroad tracks to . . . '

The revolver in Steele's hand bucked again and this time Grogan was forced to take two involuntary steps forward. Swayed, but stayed on his feet as his right shoulder spewed blood.

'You're causing this man pain, sergeant,' Steele rebuked evenly. 'Filling time with words that maybe he wanted to use.'

'Go to hell you frigging Rebs!' Grogan snarled. 'I wouldn't even tell you the last time it was I took a crap!'

'Hold your fire!' Steele snarled as Barlow and Levy went for their guns. Then, when the troopers froze in the act of drawing them, he moderated his tone. 'That was worth a try, too, captain. Getting our two hotheads angry enough to finish you quickly.'

'Damn,' Barlow muttered, while Levy looked sheepish.

'So it's going to have to be the hard way, lieutenant,' Grogan rasped. Because I'm not going to tell you a thing you want to know.'

Steele sighed through pursed lips, and pushed the revolver back into the holster. 'I believe you, captain,' he responded. Then raised his voice. 'Troopers Barlow and Levy. Get some ropes. String him up by the wrists to whatever tree branch is handy.'

'Yes, sir!' Barlow acknowledged and he and the very Jewish-looking Levy went to work with the same kind of will that sounded in the older trooper's voice.

The Virginian remained where he was, isolated from the disillusioned troopers who moved into a closer knit group as they watched the assigned men carry out the order. The two men handled the wounded Union roughly, but Grogan was able to remain stoically silent until the ropes lashed around his wrists were jerked: to wrench his arms above his head and raise him on to the toes of his feet. Then, as the weight of his entire body was felt by his bullet-holed armpits, a scream of terrible agony was vented from his gaping mouth. Which was ended when his nervous system could take no more and he fainted, his head falling forward so that his chin rested on his chest and his hat fell to the ground.

Steele, aware of the revulsion directed at him by the group of troopers, waited until the ropes had been fastened securely to the tree branch. Then ordered: 'Sergeant, have the men mount up. We're pulling out.'

'Sir!' Grady acknowledged, spitting out the single word as if it were an obscenity. Then signalled for the rest of the troop to do as the lieutenant had commanded.

'Column of two,' Steele said and moved his horse up alongside that of the non-com at the head of the short column. 'Let's go.'

No words were spoken as the troopers rode slowly out across the meadow from the edge of the trees, from one of which hung the tortured Captain Grogan. And there was just the familiar sound of hooves on muddy ground until, some fifty yards into the ridge, the Union spy came out of unconsciousness. And called: 'Lieutenant!'

Steele signalled a halt and all the men turned in their saddles to look back through the misty morning light. To where Grogan had raised his head to peer after them.

'I have something to tell you!'

The pain he was suffering could be heard in every strained word he yelled.

Steele turned his horse away from the column, but did not move the animal back toward the man on the tree.

'Last time I crapped was just before you men showed up this morning! I do it the same time every morning! Never have any trouble!'

Incredibly, genuine humour sounded in the gust of laughter that burst from the tortured man's throat.

'Crazy sonofabitch!' Barlow growled.

And neither he nor any of the other troopers were aware of the Virginian's actions until they heard the click of the carbine's hammer. A moment before Steele drew a bead on the heart of Grogan. Then squeezed the trigger.

The man on the tree spasmed once, his chin fell to his chest again, and then his form was as still as only that of a corpse can be.

'That Yankee bluebelly bastard get you riled up that time, lieutenant?' Barlow asked with a note of scorn in his voice.

'Trooper,' Grady said softly, 'that Yankee bluebelly bastard is likely the bravest man you'll ever get to meet up with.'

Steele reloaded his carbine, slid it back into the boot and resumed his position at the head of the column. Showed nothing of the self-revulsion that was welling up inside of him as he added sourly. 'That's right, sergeant. And if he's to be believed, a real regular guy.'

CHAPTER SIX

EVENTS in the shape of the Union advance overtook D Troop as they headed for Rocky Face Ridge during that day when the rain alternately lashed or fell as a drifting drizzle on the Georgia countryside. And by the time the column of ten cavalrymen came within sight of Rocky Face Ridge, the Confederate army had withdrawn, falling back south of Dalton to the town of Resaca some twelve miles down the Western and Atlantic Railroad.

A simple flanking move by Sherman's Yankees had triggered the fall back of Johnston's Rebels, but Adam Steele did not know this as, from a forward scouting position, he made a grim-faced survey of the small community of Dalton. All he saw was a concentration of Union troops and supplies, expanding by the minute, occupying a Georgia town which showed hardly a sign of battle.

And when he returned to the hollow where the troopers waited in a bedraggled group a mile or so north-east of Dalton, his feelings about what he had seen obviously showed on his face.

'It's not good, sir?' Grady asked, holding the reins of the gelding as the Virginian dismounted.

'It stinks, sergeant,' Steele answered harshly.

Their clothes heavy with rain and their flesh chilled by the day-long ride through the foul weather, the men were abruptly angry in their disappointment that warm shelter, hot food and much needed sleep in a safe place were not to be their reward.

'Aw, shit!' Barlow snarled.

'You mean we ain't gonna be able to get into town?' Trotter added.

'So even if that Yankee officer had spilled his guts, it wouldn't have made no difference at all,' Levy groaned.

This was the first time the torture and death of Captain Grogan had been mentioned by the men – at least within earshot of Lieutenant Adam Steele. Who now whirled toward the Jewish trooper and snarled: 'If war was pretty, we'd all be having a fine time, feller!'

Startled, even fearful the Virginian might lash out a blow at him, Levy staggered back several paces. And Steele immediately regretted the violent outburst directed at the man who came closest to being a kindred spirit within the troop. For during the long, wet day in the aftermath of the killing of the Union spies, the Virginian had sensed Levy was experiencing a similar degree of remorse as was he. The trooper regretting the way he had allowed himself to be infected by the evil lust for violence that was a part of the veteran Barlow's character. The lieutenant searching in vain for some kind of justification for not ending the life of Grogan as quickly as he had killed Hawkins.

It was purely coincidental that at the time of Levy's complaint and Steele's bitter retort, Sergeant Grady had handed the reins of the gelding to Barlow and stepped over to merge with the rest of the troop. Which physically set apart the two men who had displayed no sign of self-reproach from the group who were sickened by the horrifying incident, and the one guilty party who now recanted.

Few of the weary, wet, chilled, hungry and sour-tempered men in the hollow failed to take note of this division. And, his courage bolstered by the numerical odds, the normally reticent Osborne said flatly: 'This whole friggin' winter has been a friggin' waste of time and good men's lives.'

'Ain't that the truth,' Clayburn added morosely.

And there were growls of agreement.

'Not just this winter, trooper!' Steele snapped. 'You just summed up the whole damn war. Which the south is sure as hell going to lose. And there isn't a thing we can do to change that. But if there's any man wants to shorten the war for himself, now is his chance.'

'How's that, sir?' the funereal-faced Grady asked.

The Virginian pursed his lips and jerked a thumb over his shoulder. 'Around Dalton there's so many thousand Yankee soldiers I've got no way of estimating the number. Lay down your weapons here and go into Dalton and surrender. I'm making that offer to any and every man in this troop who hasn't got the guts to see this fight out to the finish.

'You can't say fairer than that, lieutenant,' Barlow rasped, as he raked his scowling eyes over the startled troopers grouped before Steele and himself.

'You I'm sure of,' the Virginian told the man beside him tersely.

'Even if you wouldn't want me to marry your sister, uh?' Barlow countered with a grin.

'You're not goin' to get any takers for that, sir,' Grady spoke up for the group, whose surprise had altered to something akin to embarrassment.

'Maybe on account that the bluebellies you surrendered to turned out to be like Mr Steele and me?' Barlow taunted.

92

The Virginian felt another impulse to anger at being compared to the vicious trooper. But reason prevailed and he grasped at the straw which the man had unknowingly given him. The obvious vindication that had eluded him throughout the day – the unsupported but surely reasonable assumption that the Union were responsible for as many atrocities as the Confederacy.

After stretched seconds of silence following Barlow's sour-voiced comment, Grady said evenly: 'For whatever reasons, sir, you still have what's left of D Troop. You have any orders you want me to give the men?'

Steele nodded. 'Have them bed down their horses and themselves, sergeant. Four hours. Two-man watch for two hour stretches. Want to be as far south as we can get before daybreak tomorrow. Maybe get some decent rest then.'

'You heard the lieutenant,' Grady snapped. 'York and Osborne first sentry duty. Then me and Trotter.' He waited until the men were engaged in attending to their horses before saying softly to Steele: 'You believe what you like, sir. I happen to think we can still win this lousy war.'

'A man's beliefs are his own business, Grady,' Steele allowed. 'Same as his hopes. And I hope you're right.'

'Somethin' I don't believe, sir.'

'What's that?'

'You ain't anythin' like Brad Barlow. Because you didn't enjoy those murders one little bit.'

'Attend to your duties, sergeant.'

During the night while the troop rested and then swung wide of Dalton and rode south, the weather improved. And so did the spirits of the men. Except for Adam Steele, who continued to be troubled by his treatment of the Union captain, as the justification he had clasped at began increasingly to ring with the hollowness of a pathetic excuse.

The good weather continued through the first half of May as D Troop paralleled the course of the Union advance southwards. Riding by day and resting through the night now, From time to time, hearing the distant crackle of gunfire whenever Yankee and Rebel skirmishers met up in the ever moving strip of railroad-bisected country between the Union advance and the Confederate retreat.

And as the men under Steele's command came to view the Rebel army tactic as a retreat rather than a withdrawal, so their spirits began to wane again: and they were torn between the desire to join the fight, perhaps to influence a reversal of Confederate fortunes, and to remain on the periphery so as not to be a part once more of a defeated army.

For his part, Steele never wavered in adhering to his original plan. The orders he had inherited from Captain Tyson were ill-founded but the troop had done what they could to put them into effect. Now, in this new situation the young lieutenant elected to use his initiative by extending the brief that General Braxton Bragg had given him. Staying clear of the massed Rebel force, which by the sound of distant gunfire had enough bands of skirmishers to serve whatever purpose General Johnston had in mind – in the hope of engaging any small group of Yankees who strayed too far out on to the left flank of the advance.

But Resaca had been taken by Sherman's armies with the same ease as Dalton before Adam Steele was given the opportunity to strike another blow at the enemy.

South of the town was the River Oostanaula which provided the first major water obstacle to the Union's push against the Confederacy. And it was from the southern bank of this river, at dawn on a day that threatened a return of bad weather, that the disillusioned troopers saw blue-garbed soldiers for the first time since the wrecking of the train.

The river marked a natural line between the high ground of the Cumberland Plateau and a broad area of flatland that stretched south and east toward another mountain range into which the railroad curved.

There was nowhere on the plain where an army the size of that commanded by Joe Johnston could make a stand and it seemed to the men of D Troop that the Rebels had run for the distant hills. Where maybe the terrain featured with the Kennesaw, Pine, Lost and Brush Mountains would provide ideal country in which Sherman's advance could be blocked. Even turned back.

But on that grey dawn, Steele and the men he commanded made their own stand against just such an isolated Yankee group as they had been waiting for since leaving the vicinity of Dalton.

It looked easy enough as the men in grey, their preparations to break camp interrupted by the sound of approaching riders, peered out of tall grass on a low rise twenty yards back from the water's edge and saw twelve blue-clad troopers emerge from a wood on the far bank of the sixty-foot wide, shallow river.

The Yankees and their mounts were weary and had obviously been riding through the night while the Rebels slept. For awhile, as a captain and lieutenant scanned the country to the south of the river with field glasses, the skirmish patrol was tense. But no threat of danger was seen and something the lieutenant said to the sergeant, corporal and eight troopers triggered a burst of laughter and signalled a time of relaxation.

A dismount was ordered, the horses were unsaddled and a fire was laid and lit. A breakfast of bacon, beans and coffee was organised while everyone, except for the cook and two troopers assigned to watch across the river, took their ease on unfurled bedrolls.

'We need this, sir,' Grady whispered to Steele as they lay, with the rest of the troop, on their bellies in the dew-damp grass.

'I know it, sergeant,' the Virginian answered.

'And it would be real nice, lieutenant,' Acting Corporal Reynolds murmured, 'if we could finish them just about the time the food and coffee is ready.'

All of D Troop had eaten nothing but cold food washed down with water since their last meal at Camp Crazy: for fear of a cooking fire giving away their presence to the enemy.

'Getting killed for a square meal is as bad as dying on an empty belly, I reckon,' Steele said. 'If they're staying, we'll wait until they're bedded down. If they're moving on, we'll hit them crossing the river.'

'Makes sense,' Barlow allowed and the comment was greeted with low grunts of agreement.

The Yankees ate breakfast, the aromas of the food and coffee drifting across the river to the nostrils of the watching Rebels. Cheroots and pipes were lit and the fire was allowed to die down. Sentry assignments were handed out and then every man except the two seated on rocks at the bank of the river stretched out on his bedroll.

An excited tension took a tentative and then a firm grip on the Rebels.

The rain held off.

The two young troopers standing the first sentry duty lost interest in the apparently empty country they were supposed to survey and moved close together. Talked for awhile, then began some kind of game with coins.

Leaving York to watch the encampment, Steele ordered the rest of the troop to where the ready-saddled mounts were waiting. And briefed the men on the plan of attack he had devised. Then he, Levy and Trotter returned to the top of the rise to join York: these four having proved themselves the best shots during the winter hunts for food on the hoof in the area of Camp Crazy.

The grizzled Brad Barlow, who had a talent for bird

mimicry learned from a half-breed army scout while serving in the far west, sounded an owl hoot to signal the rest of the troop were ready.

Steele instructed York to draw a bead on one of the sentries still playing the game while he took aim at the second.

'Trotter, the captain, Levy the lieutenant,' he rasped to the other troopers.

Hoofbeats sounded.

The trooper and the lieutenant squeezed the triggers of their carbines at the same moment as two sentries heard the horses and rose to their feet: flinging away the coins and snatching for their carbines.

Both died as their fingertips touched the stocks of the weapons. Both of them hit in the heart and spinning to the ground on the river bank.

If they made any sound of pain or warning, it was lost amid the bedlam of noise as the two shots and the thud of galloping hooves roused the sleeping men.

Grady, flanked by Barlow and Clayburn, raced his mount through the long grass and down the gentle slope to the river on the left of where the sharpshooters were hidden. At the same time as Reynolds, slightly ahead of Peck and Osborne, charged into sight on the right.

The carbines of Levy and Trotter exploded bullets across the calm surface of the water, but just one man scrambling to his feet was pitched back to the ground again: the Jewish trooper blasting a shot into the lieutenant.

'Frig it!' the ugly Trotter groaned.

'Reload, man!' Steele snarled as he and York pressed fresh rounds into the breeches of their Spencers.

And the revolvers of the six troopers in the saddle cracked out covering fire as their horses plunged into the river.

'I got the officer!' York yelled. And scored a second hit with his second shot. To send the Yankee captain rolling across the ashes of the fire in a shower of sparks.

Steele cursed under his breath and swung his carbine to the side, found a target in the sight and squeezed his trigger.

The bearded Yankee hurled his gun away and took several steps backwards before falling. But he was not hit before he got off a shot that drilled into the centre of Peck's forehead and altered the trooper's Rebel yell to a scream of horror, as the man was flung from his saddle to plunge into the white water spumed by the pumping legs of the horses.

Then Reynolds was hit. Two bullets tearing into his belly. He bent forward along his horse's neck, his booted feet were pressed out of the stirrups and he went sideways into the river.

Trotter and Levy fired and the Yankee force was reduced to five when both bullets found targets.

But a stray bullet triggered by one of these five as they whirled to race for the cover of the trees whipped through the tall grass and drilled into the skull of York while the man was rolling on to his back to make the reloading chore easier.

The fact that he felt no pain at the instant of death was evidenced by the grin of high excitement that remained fixed upon his young face as he continued to grip the carbine in one hand and the fresh bullet in the other.

'The stupid bastards ain't doin' like you said, sir!' Trotter yelled above the rattle of gunfire.

Steele looked up from the death grin on York's face to see the reason for Trotter's mixed rage and dread. And himself felt the familiar grip of ice-cold anger take hold of the entrails in his belly.

The Virginian's plan had taken account of the strong possibility that some Yankees would survive the attack and make it into the cover of the trees in back of their camp. And in this event his orders were that the horsemen should veer their mounts to the side. To gallop up and downriver as they angled for a return to the southern bank: constantly lengthening the range between themselves and the enemy while the sharpshooters directed covering fire into the timber.

But this was not how it was happening. The lone Osborne was now alongside Grady and Clayburn in a tight group behind Barlow: the veteran one-time sergeant leading the others on a course that drew a direct line between the crest of the grassy hill and the point at the edge of the timber where the Yankees had hurled themselves into cover.

For stretched seconds, Barlow and the men who had been caught up in his insane lust for killing were partially obscured by the spray kicked high into the air by the pumping hooves of their horses. Horses that dripped blood into the white water from ugly wounds in their flanks caused by the brutal use of spurs to demand greater speed.

Then men and mounts were clear of the shallow river and the troopers began to spray the trees with revolver fire as they raced across the corpse-littered campsite. In a single line of advance now, this formation hampering even more the desperate attempts of Steele, Levy and Trotter to locate targets for their loaded carbines.

There was no response from the Yankees to the incessant crackle of handgun fire by the charging troopers. And for perhaps a full second Adam Steele indulged in the wishful thought that the Union men were running scared through the wood: terrified by the slaughter of their comrades and the thirst for more killing that was exhibited in the breakneck charge out of the river and heard in the shrill Rebel yell that was vented from the throat of each man in the grip of whatever maniacal urge was driving him forward.

Levy gave voice to his own similar line of thought when, as the troopers plunged into the wood, he yelled: 'Brad Barlow and the boys are gonna finish it! It's gonna be a clean sweep of them bluebelly bastards!'

The rattle of revolver fire was abruptly mixed in with the more powerful reports of carbines being triggered. And the bloodcurdling Rebel yells were curtailed and replaced by shrieked curses.

'You wanna friggin' bet, Dave?' Trotter groaned, and dropped forward to rest his forehead on the stock of his Spencer in a gesture of despair.

'Stay alert, trooper!' Steele snarled, and returned his own gaze to the wood across the river: raking the carbine from side to side in a search for a target.

But nobody showed themselves as a hard and heavy silence descended on the smooth-flowing Oostanaula River and the country spread out from either bank. An isolated shot and a cry had ended the furious sounds of the fight with a somehow shocking abruptness: as if some huge invisible door had been closed to form an impenetrable barrier between the three men in the long grass and those who went into the timber.

'What do you think, lieutenant?' Levy asked in the lowest of whispers.

And with the speaking of these words, the apparent total silence was proved to be a trick of the mind. Steele heard the gurgling of the river, his own and the other men's breathing, the rustle of the long grass to the dictates of a slight breeze and the regular buzzing of the year's first fly feeding off the blood in York's hair.

'I reckon it's either cat and mouse or spiders and flies over there, feller,' the Virginian answered flatly, the cold anger gone now: leaving him emotionally drained with the threat of a deep depression hovering at the edges of his mind.

'Shouldn't we go . . . ' Trotter started.

Steele momentarily interrupted his intent survey of the quiet wood to glance at the bodies of Peck and Reynolds humped like dark rocks in the river. Then he replied: 'You follow the order you were given until you get another one, trooper.'

Tension stretched time as the three men waited and watched, sweat defying the chillness of the morning to stand out on their faces and moisten the palms of their hands fisted tightly around the carbines. And it seemed like an hour, but could not have been more than a few minutes when the pregnant peace of the riverside was shattered by a shout.

'Hey, you Johnnie Friggin' Rebs over there on the other side!'

'Smart spiders caught the stupid flies,' Steele rasped softly through teeth clenched between pursed lips. Swinging his carbine to draw a bead on the area where the voice emerged from the trees. But there was no movement among the brush between the trunks.

'Ain't on speakin' terms, uh?' the Union trooper shouted after several seconds had elapsed. 'Know how you feel! Me and the boys here ain't so friendly toward you!'

Trotter on his left and Levy on his right stared at Steele as if willing him to respond to the man across the river. But the Virginian remained grimly silent.

'Just want to tell you to hold your fire!' the Yankee yelled and instantly recaptured the undivided attention of the two troopers flanking the lieutenant. 'Unless you got ammo to waste on men that are already dead.' There was an interruption to the shouting and the men sprawled in the long grass strained their ears to no avail as an exchange of comments within the timber was heard as little more than growls. Then: 'Here they come, Rebs! The lucky ones!'

Hands slapped horseflesh and the animals snorted as their hooves began to beat at the ground. Brush quivered.

'No shooting unless . . . ' Steele began, but there was no need to complete the order.

'Aw, shit!' Trotter cut in.

'One's missin',' Levy said grimly.

Just three horses cantered out of the timber. In single file until they were clear of the trees, when they dispersed and slowed: wary of the many sprawled corpses and picking their way carefully between the bodies as they moved toward the bank of the river where they dipped their heads to drink. All three animals seemingly unconcerned by the dead men draped over their saddles, held in place with a booted foot in one stirrup and a hand in the other.

'Which one they got alive?' Trotter asked huskily, running the back of a hand across his eyes.

'I don't see any chevrons,' Levy answered softly.

'What you don't see is how it is,' Steele added evenly, as his eyes raked over the corpses in turn and saw that Barlow, Clayburn and Osborne had all been shot in the back. And briefly conjured up a mental image of what had happened in the timber.

The Yankee troopers were angry at the carnage the attackers had wrought, but able to think and act with cool deliberation as they threw themselves into hiding. Waiting for the hell-for-leather-riding Rebels to overshoot their positions as they pressed fresh rounds into their carbines. Then taking careful aim and squeezing the triggers. To kill three of the enemy outright.

The three lucky ones.

But what had happened to Sergeant Grady? The normally rational thinking non-com who had said at the outset: *We need this, sir* . . . and then allowed himself to be swept along with the others by the crazy impulse that blinded Barlow to everything except the need to finish the slaughter.

A man screamed. A high-pitched sound of terrible agony that brought grimaces to the faces of Steele, Levy and Trotter. And caused the horses to interrupt their drinking: all of them wheeling in the same direction and galloping along the river bank to where the mounts of Reynolds and Peck were grazing some hundred yards upstream. This as the tethered mounts of the Union troopers snorted their fear to one side of the body-littered campside.

The sound was curtailed.

'Guess you Rebs skulkin' in the long grass heard that?' the spokesman for the Yankees called.

'Those . . . '

Whatever word Trotter chose for the torturers of Grady was masked by the crack of his carbine as he triggered a wild shot across the river. Bark fragments sprayed away from a tree trunk.

'Sir, I didn't mean . . . ' the trooper started to explain.

'Reload,' Steele rasped. 'Trees are neutral but I reckon that one will live.'

Harsh laughter – from how many throats it was difficult to judge – floated across the river on the breeze.

'Figured that would get to you yellow Rebs! Ask no questions you'll get told no lies! The sarge here ain't sayin' a thing! But maybe he'll tell how many of you are over there before we hack off his other foot with this here sabre!'

For yet another stretched second nothing was heard from the timber except a low, rasping voice that did not carry. Then Grady shrieked: 'Go to hell, Yankee! The South for . . . '

Again the scream that stirred up the tethered horses, and the sounds of their distress almost covered the ending of Grady's venting of agony as he either passed out or was gagged.

'There goes the other one, Rebs!' the Union man yelled. 'And this guy certainly looks like he's got two feet in the grave!'

'Lieutenant, I can't take much more of this,' Trotter gasped.

'Right now it's not you that concerns me, feller,' Steele

snapped, his mind racing to find some way to end Grady's agony as his eyes raked over the river and its banks. Realising that any physical approach toward the men in the timber would be suicidal. He let go of the carbine to cup both hands to his mouth and shouted: 'There are just three of us! Not counting a dead man!'

There was a pause. Then: 'And five of us, Reb! Looks like the Union won this battle like most of the others! Story of the war!'

'Why'd you admit it, sir?' Levy asked in a strained voice. 'If they'd figured there were more of us they might have . . . '

He didn't know how to finish it.

The Yankee spokesman filled the gap the Jewish trooper left. 'Guess there's no chance of you guys givin' yourself up to save your sarge any more pain?'

Steele gave a fast-spoken, low-voiced order to Trotter before the Union man had finished issuing the taunt.

'Move your ass, Don,' Levy snarled, and accepted the other trooper's carbine as Trotter wriggled backwards on his belly, down the gentle slope of the grassy rise. This as Steele took a carbine from the dead York and pushed the unfired round into the breech.

'Didn't think so!' the Union man yelled, and there was a stronger strain of viciousness in his tone now. 'But you gotta wait awhile to hear what your yellowness is costin' your buddy! Bastard has gone and passed out on us! Soon as he wakes up, though . . . '

Once he was covered by the hump of the ground, Trotter had made fast time: upright and running to the horses. Then, with the reins of the mounts of Steele and Levy in one hand, he swung up into his own saddle and heeled all three animals from a standstill to a gallop.

'Milligan, they're takin' it on the lam!' a strange voice yelled. 'Let's go after the sonsofbitches!'

The Yankees had to respond with impulsive speed to the sound of the galloping horses. For the rise would shield Trotter and the two riderless animals for no more than a couple of hundred yards before the ruse was spotted as he and the horses showed.

Brush moved.

'Hold it!' the man who had done almost all the talking shouted.

One, then a second, a third and a fourth blue-uniformed man appeared at the edge of the timber, carbines in tight two-handed grips. They hesitated in response to the words.

'Be sure, trooper,' Steele warned softly, nestling his cheek against the stock of York's gun.

'You bet, lieutenant.'

'It could be a trick, you crazy . . . '

One man began to turn.

'Jesus, he's on his own!' the suspicious Yankee screamed. 'Get back in cover! There's others still – '

'Chance it!' Steele snapped.

And saw two Union men fall as the cracks of two carbines sounded as a single report.

The expended weapons were discarded and the loaded ones were snatched up.

Steele's target was still in full view as he made to plunge through the brush. A bullet drilling into his back, left of centre, sent him crashing forward with greater speed.

Levy's man was out of sight, but the trooper had the line of his attempted escape and he showed a tight grin of confidence in his ability as he exploded a shot.

'You sonsofbitches, you sonsofbitches!' the spokesman shrieked, rage sending his tone to a shrillness that was almost feminine. 'I'll kill him, I'll kill him, I'll kill him!'

The two Confederates on the hill crest loaded one carbine apiece. Then froze, staring intently across the river, over the bodies of their latest victims and into the dense brush. From which, after the rage-maddened voice had ceased to vent the threat, came the sickening sounds of sabre lashing into human flesh.

Had the severing of Grady's feet not been boasted of, perhaps Steele and Levy would not have recognised the dull thudding for what it was. But each scowling man knew there could be no mistake about the mind picture which was conjured up so vividly.

'Let's go, trooper,' Steele said, and took Trotter's carbine as well as his own as he bellied backwards down from the top of the rise. This after the final blow had been wielded against the flesh of Sergeant Grady: who had probably been dead a full thirty seconds before the mutilation was ended.

'Why him, sir?' Levy asked as they waited at the foot of the rise on the blind side from the last survivor of the Union patrol: looking toward Trotter who was bringing the horses back.

'Who the hell can answer that?' Steele replied irritably.

'It oughta have been Brad Barlow.'

The horses were there and the trooper and the officer swung up into their saddles. The carbines were thrust into the boots. Trotter eyed Levy quizzically.

'How's that, Dave?'

'Somehow it wouldn't have seemed so bad if it had been Barlow gettin' a taste of the kinda medicine he liked to dish out,' the Jew muttered bitterly.

'I heard the shootin', lieutenant,' Trotter said. 'Did it work?'

'Four of them killed, feller,' Steele answered as he signalled a wheel and gallop. 'Left one of them mad enough to finish Grady.'

When they were out of the cover of the rise, a gunshot sounded behind him. Then another. And another.

But the trio of Confederate riders did not glance back or

take any evasive action: relied on the speed of the gallop and the disturbed state of the Yankee to ensure that every shot from a succession of dead men's guns went wide of the targets.

Then the range was too long and the Union trooper realised it. Abandoned his effort to take vengeance against the rapidly diminishing riders.

Steele slowed the pace to an easy walk and it would have been possible to talk. But nobody said anything for a long time as each man thought his own thoughts about the slaughter at the river.

Until Trotter said: 'I don't think that's right what you said about it bein' better if it was Barlow, Dave.'

'Uh?' Levy grunted absently.

'I wouldn't want that kinda thing to happen to my worst enemy, even.'

Levy sighed. 'Maybe you're right, Don. Only way to think of it is there but for the grace of God . . . ' He shrugged.

'And be grateful it wasn't us had to give the order that sent all those guys . . . ' He allowed the sentence to hang. Then added quickly: 'I ain't knockin' you for doin' it, lieutenant. Just sayin' how much I appreciate bein' just an ordinary trooper.'

'Relax, feller,' the Virginian drawled. 'Command has its privileges, too. And maybe I'll get some of them one day.'

'Hell, let's look on the bright side,' Levy growled. 'That bluebelly was crowin' one time about it bein' another Yankee victory. But they was twelve and lost eleven. We were ten and lost seven.'

'And nobody gained a friggin' thing!' Trotter complained bitterly, a scowl fixed on his homely face.

'Except maybe a little learning,' Steele added. 'About the luck – good and bad – of the draw.'

CHAPTER SEVEN

THROUGHOUT May and into June Sherman's advance which the Yankees called Operation Crusher continued to push the Rebel army of General Johnston further and further back to what was obviously the Union's intended destination – Atlanta.

During this period Sherman made use of the railroad to transport men and supplies: and the towns of Calhoun, Adairsville and Kingston, then Cartersville, the Etowah River Crossing and Allatoona fell easily into Yankee hands. Skirmishes followed, few of which were on a much larger scale than the one D Troop had instigated at the Oostanaula River.

But then the Union forsook the railroad and began to use wagon trains for transportation. And the advance was slowed and finally ground to a halt. For by early June the unusually heavy spring rains falling upon the red clay of Georgia has turned the roads into quagmires in which men and horses sank knee-deep, and heavily laden wagons settled to their wheelhubs.

The Union needed time to revert to rail transport. And

while they took it, the Rebels made use of the respite to fortify the wooded slopes of Kennesaw Mountain – less than twenty miles north of Atlanta.

Elsewhere the tides of war ebbed and flowed for both sides. The Battles of the Wilderness and Spotsylvania Courthouse were fought in Virginia. Then Cold Harbor, Virginia and Brice's Crossroads, Mississippi, were the scenes of other pitched battles. The Union began the siege of Petersberg, Virginia. And, most distant of all, there was an incident that caused international rumblings in diplomatic circles when, off the French seaport of Cherbourg, a Union warship attacked and sank the Rebel raider *Alabama*.

Throughout all this fighting and suffering and dying, conflicting claims to victory were made. But few of the results were as clear-cut as the sinking of one vessel by another. And the battles fought on American soil served little more purpose than to prolong the war.

Lieutenant Adam Steele, and troopers Dave Levy and Don Trotter had no way of knowing what turns the war was taking in other parts of the country. Nor, as they continued to ride south through almost constant rain, could they be aware of the precise details of what was happening in the theatre of operations that included themselves.

Distant gunfire was more sporadic now. And some days they did not hear any exchange of shots. So from this it seemed reasonable to assume the Union advance was slowing – but for some reason other than a determined defensive stand by the Rebels. Because the trio of cavalrymen had certainly not heard the unmistakable sounds of a full-scale pitched battle.

And they did not hear such until a little after nine o'clock on the morning of June 27.

It was raining again, but no longer cold. The three troopers were sweating under the weight of their protective clothing. And fretting morosely as yet another day of aimless travel stretched out before them.

Then a bugle call sounded through the regular clop of hooves and the hiss of the falling rain. The riders halted their mounts in unison, cocking their heads and straining their ears to get a bearing on the direction from which the sound came. And the distance it was travelling. A cannon roared and the shell whistled through the air. But before the crash of it striking a target reached the ears of the unmoving men in the saddles, a whole battery of heavy artillery arced a hail of death into the morning. No more than half a mile ahead of the troopers.

'Welcome back to the war, men,' Steele rasped as, like Levy and Trotter, he stroked the neck of his horse, all the animals made uneasy by the cacophony of battle which they had not heard for so long. 'Let's go.'

The attack signalled by the bugler and opened by the cannonading was forward and to the right of the troopers. And as they spurred their mounts into a canter an answering salvo was exploded from forward and to the left. Which indicated the Union had initiated the fight and at long last the Rebels were in a position to counter the men in blue.

For stretched minutes as the troopers rode closer to the battleground, veering toward the Confederate positions, the exchange of heavy ordnance fire provided the only sounds of the engagement to reach them. Then, as they approached the railroad and Steele experienced a sense of satisfaction that his map reading had been accurate – the track was exactly where he expected it to be beyond the towering height of Brush Mountain – the big guns ceased their pounding. And the crackle of small-arms took over, interspersed with the battle cries of men.

'Over there, lieutenant?' Levy yelled, pointing with a trembling hand toward a small single-storey house at the side of the railroad.

Steele acknowledged the suggestion by wrenching on his

reins to veer the gelding in the direction of the house. Up and over the track. Through the open gateway and into the neat garden fronting the house: the hooves of the horses crushing carefully planted flowers in their beds and churning ugly scars in the neatly trimmed lawn. Leaping from the saddles, drawing the carbines from the boots. Hitching the reins to the rail that skirted the white-painted stoop. Whatever sounds they made totally masked by the din of an infantry charge against an obviously entrenched enemy. A flank of the battle no more than a few hundred feet away from the house, on a rocky and densely timbered slope.

Steele kicked open the door and followed it into the pleasant parlour. Where a plain-faced young woman with a baby in her arms cowered back in a chair, shocked into a frozen posture by the violent entrance of the Virginian – obviously aware for the first time that strangers were intruding into her home.

'Beg pardon, ma'am,' Steele said as Trotter and Levy came to a halt beside him, all of them dripping rainwater on to the carpet.

'Please . . . ' the woman whispered, clutching the baby more tightly to her breasts, ' . . . don't harm us.'

'Anyone else in the house, lady?' Trotter demanded.

She shook her head, the trooper's harsh tones raising a deeper fear into her wide eyes. 'My father . . . he went to watch the fightin'. There's just the three of us live here.' Tears squeezed from the corners of her eyes and ran down her pallid cheeks. 'We support the Cause. My husband, he died at Gettysbury without seein' the son he fathered. Please don't harm us.'

Her eyes raked back and forth over the faces of all three troopers.

Steele whirled. 'Outside! We don't need this place!'

He took the lead and heard the first sob of relief vented

by the woman before he crossed the stoop and raced around to the rear of the house. Vegetables grew in the large backyard and for several paces he found himself stepping carefully to avoid trampling them. But then the dangerous closeness of the fighting – he could now hear the crack of bullets through the air and their impact with trees and rocks – blocked his mind to everything save joining the battle and surviving it.

He was first to pass the privy and vault over the picket fence that marked the rear boundary of the property. Then remained in the lead up a steep, brush-covered embankment. Crouched low as he climbed, having to trust to blind luck that the bullets criss-crossing the hillside went wide of him and the two cursing troopers hard on his heels.

In a shallow hollow where the men threw themselves to regain their breath, Levy gasped: 'I figure we're caught in the damn middle, lieutenant. Seems like lead is comin' from every which way.'

Trotter jerked a thumb southwards. 'Our boys are over there, right sir?'

'Reckon so,' the Virginian agreed, then held up a hand to command silence.

The troopers complied, and then lost their quizzical expressions as they realised what had captured Steele's attention.

The closest Rebel guns were being exploded maybe a hundred and fifty yards to the south. The shots triggered by men moving neither forwards nor backwards from positions high on the lower slopes of a mountain. While the Yankees were steadily narrowing the gap to where the Confederates were entrenched. But they were still at least a quarter of a mile to the north of where the trio crouched in the hollow, listening to a rifle that blasted out a shot at about fifteen second intervals, triggered by somebody no more than twenty or thirty feet higher up the embankment.

'One of us or one of them?' Trotter posed at length.

'Let's try not to get our heads blown off finding out,' Steele answered. And signalled that they should begin climbing again.

Up through brush that snagged at their clothing and whipped at their faces. Around a rocky projection and between the spindly trunks of some saplings, to emerge on to a level shelf at the top of the embankment. At the farther side of which a man in dungarees sat on his haunches, methodically loading, aiming and firing a Sharps rifle. An elderly man with grey hair and heavily wrinkled skin. Short and thin, but handling the big calibre rifle with the ease of long experience, absorbing its recoil and rasping: 'Damn you!' after each triggering of a shot.

In front of him was a line of ragged rock that provided excellent cover which for the moment was unnecessary. For no reply came to the monotonously regular shots he triggered from out of his natural fortification. Shots which were aimed either across or down the slope – at the advancing Union men.

Despite this, though, Steele, Levy and Trotter advanced warily over the shelf: carbines levelled. For although the old-timer was calm enough in the way he sharpshot at the Yankees, to be surprised by the abrupt appearance of three soldiers might blind him to the colour of their uniforms. Particularly when these uniforms were sodden to a darker hue by the downpour.

The civilian exploded another shot from the sharps and muttered: 'Damn you!'

From twenty feet away, Steele announced: 'You're doing a fine job, feller.'

The man did not turn his head. Without shifting his attention from the terrain on the other side of the rocky wall, he ejected the empty shellcase, reached for a fresh round from a box at his side and pushed it into the breech.

'Not just the gunfire, sir,' Levy said, as loudly as Steele had spoken. 'He's deaf as a post, I figure.'

The troopers had halted. They waited for the man to get off another shot and add his curse. Then closed in on him, crouching so as not to show themselves above the jagged top of the natural rampart.

Steele signalled to Trotter, who nodded and reached out to fist a hand around the old man's wrist as he sought another fresh shell. The old timer screamed 'damn you!' now as the speed of his turn toppled him to the ground and he stared in boundless hatred at the trooper.

'Tell him he's okay!' the Virginian snapped as, with Levy at his side, he surveyed the slope and a broad gin of pleasure spread across his face.

The Yankees were taking a beating in what had all the earmarks of a suicidal assault upon unassailable Rebel positions. It was like Lookout Mountain all over again, except that here on the heights of Kennesaw the Confederates were not about to be driven back. For during the period of bad weather which had stalled the Union move south, Joe Johnston's men had improved on the natural bastion that the mountain terrain provided. And were now in trenches and behind stout timber breastworks which looked to Steele to have been virtually untouched by the Yankee artillery barrage which had opened the battle.

Unlike the Union's base camp on the low ground. Which had taken a battering from the Rebel big guns. For down there, despite the rain which still poured from the grey sky, a dozen fires blazed, giving off clouds of billowing black smoke. As the smoke shifted to the dictates of the gentle wind, various component parts of the entire scene of carnage were revealed.

Overturned cannons. Crippled wagons. Dead horses. Many more dead bodies. What was left of tent canvas, flapping on poles. Two tattered Stars and Stripes trampled into the mud.

Through this smoke-laden, fire-lighted wreckage blue-clad forms continued to run: ordered into the assault to replace the many dead at the base of the hill and on the high ground. Confidently eager to join the fight and moving to the limit of their strength until the incline slowed them. Then they came within range of the Rebel carbine fire and the urge to survive swamped that to avenge the slaughter of their comrades.

Here and there corpsmen hurried from one patch of insubstantial cover to another. To locate the wounded, lay them on litters and return downhill to the waiting ambulances.

'It sure makes a man feel good,' Levy said enthusiastically as he and Steele had completed the fast survey of the situation. And both of them swung around to look at the old-timer who was still cursing them.

'Listen!' Steele yelled.

'My daugher! My daughter and her kid! What'd you bastards do to them? You come up from the house! It's the only way up to here!'

'Listen, frig you!' the Virginian roared, caught hold of the man's shoulder and shoved him out full-length on to his back. Held him there with the carbine barrel across his throat: as he kneeled over him, snatched off his cap and pushed it close to the man's face. So he could see the insignia. Confederates, see?'

'Soldiers is all the same and . . .'

'Steele used the cap to beat the man on both cheeks several times. Until he choked off what he was yelling and ceased to struggle against the pressure of the gun barrel.

'You're deaf?' the Virginian asked, making sure to pronounce the words clearly and overemphasising the movement of his lips.

'But a long ways from bein' blind.'

'You read lips?'

'Damn right, mister!'

'Well read mine, feller.'

'All right to take up where the crazy old fool left off, Lieutenant?' Trotter asked.

'Get to it,' Steele answered, turning his face away from that of the old man as he did so. Then, enunciating as clearly as before, he assured: 'The woman and baby in the house are all right, feller. You did a good job up here. But now we're taking over. Best thing you can do it go down and take them out of the house. In case the Confederacy pulls back and the Yankees find out how much you hate them.'

Anger had departed from the old man's eyes, to be replaced by distrust. He nodded, and snarled: 'If you let me up, mister, I'm sure as hell goin' back to the house. Cause I ain't gonna believe a word you say until I seen with my own eyes it's true.'

'Get to it,' Steele invited, raising the Spencer and replacing his cap: swinging away from the man to take a place alongside Trotter and Levy behind the low rock wall.

'Like blastin' at apples in a barrel!' the ugly Trotter yelled in high enjoyment as he triggered a shot across the slope. 'And them bluebellies ain't got no idea anyone's up here!'

He was right. For as blue-uniformed men continued to move up the slope, it was into a hail of bullets poured down at them from behind the Rebel defences high on the mountainside. And since the firing was incessant and the din deafening, the relatively few shots exploding out from behind the ramparts to the attackers' left went unnoticed. Except, too late, by the men who were hit and pitched to the rain-sodden ground. While the Yankees who scrambled over or around their fallen comrades were too intent upon reaching the known positions of the massed Rebel force to notice that every now and then a fatal bullet cracked across the line of advance rather than directly into it.

But it was too good a situation to last and while he took as much advantage of it as the pair of troopers, Steele was aware of the danger of being outflanked. For shots had been traded between the attackers and the defenders while he led the men up the embankment from the house. Which meant that the position they occupied was not far enough out on the Union's left flank to be entirely safe: and that, if there was a lull in the shooting battle, there was a strong possibility of Yankees moving stealthily forward to find this pocket of cover from which so many of their number had been gunned down.

'Enough!' he yelled at length.

'What the hell?' Trotter demanded as he swung the Spencer to track a running man and triggered a shot which sent the Union soldier pitching to the side and then rolling down the hill.

'Sir?' Levy asked, ready to be as angry as the ugly trooper.

'We're leaving!' the Virginian said grimly. 'We'll get the horses and swing as wide as we need to get behind our own lines.'

Steele had backed off from the natural wall and risen to his full height. On hearing his order and snapping their responses, the two troopers turned just their heads to stare at him. But now they looked beyond him and their new-born anger changed in an instant to fear. This as they flung down their empty carbines and fumbled for the holstered revolvers.

'Watch out, sir!' Levy shouted.

'What the hell?' Trotter yelled at the same moment.

And Steele whirled, having recognised from their change of expression that there was a threat in back of him.

'You lyin' bastard!' the dungaree-clad old man shrieked as he lunged across the shelf of rock toward the Virginian, every fibre of his slightly built frame trembling with hatred while his time-worn face betrayed a degree of exhaustion close to total collapse.

But however much energy he had used in scrambling up the hill from the house, he was able to summon sufficient to power a final turn of speed to close the gap on the surprised lieutenant.

The old and the young man collided and for part of a second Adam Steele experienced a boundless sense of terror at the awesome strength of the old man as the thin arms embraced him in a powerful bearhug, virtually paralysing him as both of them crashed to the ground.

The Spencer with an expended round in the breech slipped from Steele's gloved hand. And it was impossible for him to break the vice-like hold of the man's arms and reach for the holstered Dance Brothers revolver. Impossible too, for either Levy or Trotter to risk a shot which might hit the lieutenant as the two men rolled one way and then another on the ground: as the old-timer sought to crush Steele to death and the Virginian struggled to bring up his right knee and reach for the knife in the boot sheath.

While, all the time, the crazed man drawing upon the seemingly limitless strength of insanity, repeated time and time again: 'Why'd you do it, you bastard? Why'd you do it, you bastard?'

Then, abruptly, it was over.

Not content with the time it was taking to squeeze the life out of the helpless Steele, the old man had begun to smash his head into the side of his victim's face. Three times the Virginian felt the pain of the blows as the man's brow crashed against his cheekbone. Also felt the wet warmth of blood on his cheek as the skin split. And it was this that triggered a surge of anger that supplied the will and strength to break free of the bearhug. An instant before fate ordained that the struggle was to be ended.

Both men were on their sides and Levy and Trotter were stooping to drag the old-timer away from Steele. The Virginian forced an arm away from his side and the old man's hands were torn apart – as he head-butted once more.

For a moment, it seemed that the scream which was vented from the ancient throat was caused by despair. But then the sound was curtailed and he rolled over on to his back and became utterly still. The rain beating down on his face diluted the beads of crimson blood that squeezed like coloured tears from the corner of his closed right eye.

'What happened?' the ugly Trotter asked huskily as, like Steele who was rising painfully to his feet, he stared at the insipidly coloured mixture of rain and blood running across the sunken cheek of the dead man.

'Your collar, sir,' Levy muttered.

The Virginian and Trotter shifted their attention to that portion of the tunic which was fascinating Levy. And saw that, during the death struggle, the collar was turned down and the point and most of the length of the pearl-headed stickpin taken from the Union captain at the train wreck protruded outwards. Just before the rain washed off a final bead of red, the pin showed the evidence that, as the old man attempted a final head-butt, the pin speared his eye. Obviously sinking in deep enough to pierce the brain.

'Man, that's incredible!' Trotter gasped

'Learn by it,' Steele growled, wincing at the pain in his chest from the bearhug as he withdrew the pin, rearranged the tunic collar and re-inserted it. 'Don't get too close to a man unless you can see his point.'

Out on the lower slopes of Kennesaw Mountain the battle continued unabated in the teeming rain.

'Sir, we gonna . . . ' Levy started.

Steele watched the brush from which the old-timer had emerged, as he picked up his Spencer and opened the breech.

'Reload,' he instructed. 'My last order stands.'

'Yeah, Dave,' Trotter muttered, gripped by the same brand of tension that infected Steele. 'Somethin' happened down the hill that stirred up that crazy old guy.'

'Keep the noise down,' Steele rasped, and began to backtrack along the way he had led the troopers up the slope, ears strained and eyes constantly moving in their sockets – carbine held loosely in a double-handed grip.

Through the brush, between the saplings and around the rocky projection. Then down into the hollow where they had paused for breath. Now they stopped to concentrate on listening and watching for unknown danger.

Bullets no longer cracked through the rain-washed air over their heads – maybe to indicate that Steele's anxiety about being surrounded atop the embankment had been unfounded. Alternatively to warn that the Yankees on this section of the hill had not been beaten back: instead were silently waiting in hiding for the result of the old-timer's scramble to the top of the embankment.

'Sir!' Levy rasped in a strained whisper, pointing.

'I see it,' Steele answered in the same tone.

What held the attention of all three men was a covered wagon being hauled by a struggling team of four horses: was watched by them for perhaps a half minute as it slithered past a gap in the trees to the north of the house beside the railroad. They continued to watch the same spot for another half minute as the hoofprints and wheelruts in the mud were obliterated by rain. But nothing and nobody showed there.

'Let's get closer,' the Virginian growled and bellied up over the rim of the hollow, sliding easily through the mud.

At the foot of the embankment they crouched in the brush, just outside the fence enclosing the back yard of the neat, well-tended house. The teeming rain and the din of the

120

battle for the mountain continued to be the only sounds which reached their ears.

They climbed the fence and paused again, pressed close together in the scant cover of the foul smelling privy. Eyed each other tensely when a man shouted something. Horses snorted. Wagon timbers creaked.

'They'll see our mounts, sir,' Trotter croaked, as if only now did he recall that the three animals had been left hitched to the stoop of the house.

'Reckon they've already been seen, trooper,' Steele murmured.

He pointed to the right and moved in that direction, crouching low as he skirted the fence. Then threw himself full-length to the ground when a fusillade of gunshots cracked out.

'Oh, Christ!' Trotter groaned as he and Levy followed the Virginian down.

Then, moments later, all three realised the shots were not aimed at them: raised their heads and used their elbows to propel themselves forward. Hearing the gunfire, the yells, the screams and the cries at the sounds of a skirmish taking place to the front and other side of the house.

They reached the corner of the fence and turned it. Scrambled forward to a point where they had a clear view of what was happening.

The Union wagon had been brought to a halt, one of the team heaped inertly on the ground and the other three horses struggling vainly to get free of the traces. Two blue-uniformed forms were folded backwards over the wagon seat. Three more were sprawled across the railroad track beside the stalled wagon. While at least a dozen more Yankees who had been escorting the vehicle were alive and in cover: pouring a hail of gunfire at the house from which the ambush had been sprung.

'Follow me!' Steele snapped and rose and whirled to

lunge back along the fence to the rear corner, around it and toward the privy. Past this and into the timber to the north of the house. Not glancing to see if the troopers were with him after he had crashed between them at the start of the move.

Bullets continued to crack out of the house and to thud into its timber walls. None came close to him.

He slowed his pace, trading speed for stealth among the trees. He transferred the carbine to his left hand and drew the Dance Brothers revolver. Now looked over his shoulder as a twig cracked. Saw the breathless Levy and Trotter had complied with the order. Raised the barrel of the handgun to his lips like a finger to signal the need for silence. Then used the revolver to send Trotter to the left and Levy to the right. Started directly forward himself.

The gunfire was incessant, virtually masking out the sounds of the major struggle taking place on the slope beyond the embankment. But orders had been given and received by the Yankees in the wake of the ambush. And the unfortunate Union soldiers sent to flank the house walked into yet another trap.

There were six of them, moving through the trees at a run: eager to get to positions from which they could hit the enemy unexpectedly. And not realising danger was so close at hand until Steele, Trotter and Levy triggered their carbines.

Three of the blue-clad forms were halted in their tracks and corkscrewed to the ground with red stains blossoming on the fronts of their tunics. While the other three had time only to glance in horror at their falling comrades before the Rebels fired their revolvers: while rising or swinging into sight from brush and tree trunks.

Just one of the Union men triggered a shot, and this was an instinctive squeezing of a finger as the man fell backwards – the bullet exploding skywards. Of the other two, one dropped instantly dead with a shot in his heart. The other received a flesh wound in the side and made to turn and run back to where he had come from. Discarding his carbine and venting a wail of terror.

Three revolvers tracked his moves and then were fired at the same instant.

'Heeellllpp!' he screamed as he fell headlong with a trio of ugly holes in his back.

'You're past that,' Trotter snarled. And gaped his mouth wide to shriek the Rebel yell as he plunged forward, leaping over the fallen Yankees.

'Trooper!' Steele bellowed.

'Don, don't be crazy!' Levy roared.

But the man was deaf to the words and perhaps all his sensibilities were numbed to all outside influences while he submitted to the reckless euphoria of completing the victory.

'Let's go!' Steele called to Levy, and powered in the wake of Trotter, knowing from experience the brand of insanity that was gripping the ugly trooper.

For he had acted thus on more than one occasion during the war: in response to an unstoppable desire to bring vengeance against an enemy responsible for so much carnage, in reaction to real or imagined blunders by his own high command, or to release pent up emotion that had accumulated over a long period of relative inactivity. But whatever the trigger, the instinct which was given rein was that of a man who has killed and needs desperately to kill again. No matter what the risk to himself.

Trotter was out of sight. But the Rebel yell could be heard by Steele and Levy. And the crackle of his revolver.

'Shit, why not!' Levy roared, and added his voice to the Confederate battlecry.

For perhaps three full seconds Adam Steele remained rational in his thinking: totally aware of the stupid risks he and the troopers were running. Then he gaped his lips wide to shriek the bloodcurdling sound which had been a feature of every major battle he had fought in.

Crouching up on the top of the embankment behind the rock ramparts, the killing had been too easy. Too cold-blooded. With no more danger attached to it than when he had executed Hawkins and put Grogan out of his misery. Or when, from the cover of the long grass on the hill crest, they had opened fire on the Yankees camped across the river.

When a man killed in such a way, there was certainly a sense of satisfaction to see the enemy fall through the blurring effect of the muzzle smoke. But that sensation could not be compared with the pleasure – the exhilaration – of charging flat out at the enemy, possibly in full view of them. Knowing the odds were fifty-fifty against you or the other man surviving.

It had nothing to do with fair play for you did not give the other man a chance for his sake. You did it for the purely selfish reason of heightening your own enjoyment.

Which was insane.

But then, in the cold light of calm, rational thinking, war was insane.

Steele and Levy gained on and drew level with Trotter: all three triggering shots from their revolvers into the timber ahead of them. Running and firing blindly in the direction where men were shouting and other gunfire was crackling.

Rebel and Yankee bullets cracked, whined and thudded into trees. And for long moments the shooting from the house was curtailed.

Then the three surviving members of D Troop burst upon the Union positions beside the stalled wagon. And their revolvers were empty of live rounds.

One Yankee was dead behind the brush that was their cover. Another was in bad shape with a belly wound. Five others were momentarily surprised. Not by the appearance of the three mud-spattered, killer-grinning Rebels. But by the fact that there were only three of them.

Momentum drove the Confederates forward. First hurling their empty revolvers at the enemy, then swinging their carbines like clubs. So that they were among and upon the Union men before the Yankees recovered.

A fusillade of gunshots exploded from the house and the curses that ripped from the mouths of Steele, Trotter and Levy were as much for the men there as the Yankees who now began to fight back.

Steele heard the sickening crack of a skull splitting as he laid the Spencer barrel across the side of a corporal's head.

Trotter sent a lieutenant sprawling with a whiplash blow of his carbine across the man's shoulder blades.

Levy missed with his carbine turned club, and fell down, going under the bullet fired by another Yankee.

Steele hurled his Spencer at the man with the revolver before he could cock and fire the Colt again. Which gave Levy time to roll, half raise and thrust his carbine muzzle hard into the Yankee's crotch. Then the Virginian dived full-length for another Union soldier who had drawn a bead on him – but had forgotten to cock his Colt.

In mid-air, the Rebel officer bent the knee of his right leg, drew the knife from the sheath inside the gaping slit, and swung his arm in a wide and powerful arc. To sink the blade to the hilt in the left side of the young Yankee's neck. Which was deep enough so that the bloodied point of the knife emerged from the right side.

'Lieutenant!' Levy shrieked and Steele let go of the deeply implanted knife and rolled away from the victim who was toppling sideways from his sitting posture.

A carbine exploded close to him and he felt the rush of air as the bullet cracked within a fraction of an inch of his cheek. Just for a moment the killer grin left his face. But reappeared when he saw it was the man with the gut wound who had fired at him: and was now in a state of panic as he fumbled to eject the spent shellcase and reload.

The Virginian reached into his tunic pocket, hearing a thudding in his ears as he drew out the tiny Remington.

'Just him left, sir!' Trotter yelled happily.

The gunfire from the house had stopped.

Stretched flat out on his belly, Steele aimed the under-and-over at the wounded and terrified Union sergeant. And it seemed to him the man took a very long time to get the carbine loaded and cocked.

'Oh, my God!' the non-com gasped, and allowed the carbine to sag, his attention having been drawn away from Steele and the aimed Remington. His eyes becoming fixed upon something that was happening behind and to the Virginian's left.

'Go see him, feller,' Steele rasped through teeth clenched between drawn-back lips in an evil and brutal grin. Then squeezed the trigger of the small gun to tunnel a bullet through the centre of the wounded man's forehead.

When the crack of the Remington's shot no longer rang in his ears, the thudding in his head had also stopped. There was just the hiss of the teeming rain and the heavy breathing of himself and the two troopers in the brush: against the somehow muted sounds of the battle on the hill beyond the timber and the embankment.

He got up on to all fours, then came erect, intending to retrieve his knife and Spencer and Dance Brothers revolver. But first he spared a glance for the grey-uniformed men emerging on to the stoop of the house. Men who began to shout at him. But he ignored them to look down at a man sprawled on his back, unmoving, between the deep breathing, still grinning Trotter and Levy.

The man was dead and he had no face. There was just a crimson pulp where once features had given him individuality.

The two Rebel troopers were smiling down at the mess of the Yankee's head, the rain washing blood from the stocks of the carbines which had obviously thudded time and time again against the defenceless flesh of the man on the ground.

Levy saw Steele watching and he nudged Trotter. Both men ended their smiles, but whereas Levy looked sheepish, Trotter was defiant.

'It's like Sergeant Grady said at the river, sir. We needed that. Dave and me, we needed this.'

'Did I say anything?' the Virginian countered evenly.

The ten soliders who had run out of the house as the skirmish drew to a close now came to a halt. Some at the wagon and others to survey the results of the slaughter in the brush.

'Beg pardon, sir, but where did you come from?' a sergeant asked as he stood to attention and saluted.

'Lookout Mountain,' Steele answered wearily, as he rested a booted foot on the head of the Union sergeant: and needed to exert a great deal of strength to pull the knife from the man's neck.

'But that was months ago, sir.'

'Only that long? Seems like years.' He claimed his Spencer carbine and the Dance Brothers revolver. Heard a Union soldier groan, and asked the perplexed sergeant: 'You have facilities for taking prisoners?'

'Yes, sir.'

'Then take them, sergeant.'

'I'll arrange it, sir.' The non-com had abandoned his attempts to work out for himself an explanation for the presence of the trio of kill-crazy cavalrymen. Now issued orders to the privates behind him, then: 'Captain Carey's compliments, sir. He's in bad shape at the house. Asked me to find out what was happening here.'

Steele's expression of weariness was momentarily displaced by a look akin to disappointment. Which did not go unnoticed by Levy and Trotter. Who in turn expressed something close to sympathy for the lieutenant.

It was the ugly trooper who growled: 'When we got here, you said welcome back to the war, sir. Guess now it's a matter of welcome back to the army.'

'Come on, sergeant,' Steele muttered, starting toward the house as, over on the slope of Kennesaw Mountain, the din of battle diminished.

The non-com swallowed hard and asked tentatively as he drew level with the Virginian: 'Lieutenant, what did that man mean? You and them haven't . . . you didn't, after Lookout Mountain go . . . ' He took a deep breath: 'You been out of the war since . . . '

'We aren't deserters, feller,' Steele cut in. 'Just that we've had a chance to serve the Cause without treating the service as a religion.'

The sergeant shook his head, his perplexity increasing. 'You lost me again, sir.'

'We're opposed to taking orders.'

CHAPTER EIGHT

THE first man Steele saw when he crossed the stoop and entered the no longer neat and tidy house was Cliff Gordon, his erstwhile friend and often class war enemy from their home town of Keysville.

The chevrons on his tunic sleeve showed that he had made corporal. The drying blood on the side of his head and the utter stillness of his beefily built frame showed that he was dead. One of four men who had been left where they died during an engagement which Rebel army records would account a success.

'That you, Sergeant Gilmore?' a man called weakly from another room as Steele shifted his cold-eyed gaze from Gordon to the other corpses, to the bloodstains, the bullet holes, the overturned furniture and the smashed bric-à-brac.

'Yes, sir!' Gilmore supplied, and ushered Steele across the room. Murmured: 'We made the captain as comfortable as we could. But he won't last long.'

The Virginian stepped into an alcove to one side of the fireplace. An open doorway to left and right gave on to bedrooms. A man with captain's insignia on his tunic was sprawled on his back on a bed in the spartanly furnished room to the right. Feminine frills and bright colours distinguished the room to the left. The plain-faced woman lay along the centre of the big double bed in there. Her baby lay in the crook of her right arm. Bloodstains showed more evilly bright on the child's white shawl than on the darker hued dress of its mother.

Nothing of the icy depths of Steele's anger showed on his impassive face as he turned his back on the dead woman and baby and entered the other bedroom to ask evenly: 'How did it happen, feller?'

Carey had been hit twice. Once in the thigh and again higher up. His pants leg from the crotch to the right knee was soaked with bright crimson. The knowledge of his impending death showed in every line of his wan face.

'You'll address me as captain, lieutenant!' the senior officer snapped, able to turn his head on the pillow but not to raise it.

Steele halted beside the bed, gripping the mud-spattered carbine tightly in both gloved hands. 'I'll address you to hell and send you there before your time if you're responsible for killing that woman and her child.'

Carey's pain-filled eyes were trapped by the unblinking gaze of Steele's cold stare. He swallowed hard before he was able to speak: 'Mister, consider yourself . . . '

'Easy, captain,' Gilmore interrupted anxiously as he reached the bed beside Steele, and glared a tacit rebuke at the Virginian. 'It won't do you no good to get that way.' Then, fast to the hate and anger-filled man at his side, 'We got orders to circle around this side of the mountain and check if the Yankees was tryin' to flank us. Reached this house and saw the three cavalry mounts hitched outside. Moved in like we was walkin' on eggs. But didn't appear to be nobody inside. Got the word from a scout that some Yankees were headin' this way with a wagon. Hid the horses and fixed to hit the Yankees hard.'

He paused for breath, and anguish rather than agony shone dully in the captain's eyes now as he turned his head on the pillow to try to look between Steele and Gilmore: through the two open doorways and into the other bedroom.

'We heard a noise,' the non-com went on, more slowly now, his tone a match for the emotion shown on Carey's wan face. 'Out in the kitchen. The captain sent Corporal Gordon and Trooper Harvey to check on it. And we expected the Yankees to show up around the timber any second.'

Gilmore paused again. Not for breath this time. Steele glanced at his face and saw that memories were punishing him as severely as they were the captain.

'Carry on, sergeant,' Carey rasped.

'Heard a baby cry, sir.' Gilmore sounded as if he was about to throw up. 'Then it stopped. And a woman started to scream. The captain ordered the men in the kitchen to quieten the noise. And the woman stopped screamin'. Oh, my God . . . '

Carey stared fixedly up at Steele again. 'The way Corporal Gordon reported it, lieutenant, they opened the door of the larder and the woman had a carving knife to the baby. When she saw the two men pointing their weapons at her, she thrust the knife home. Started to scream. The corporal acted on my order and used his own knife to stab the woman to death. It was necessary because she was not quick enough to withdraw the knife from her baby and kill herself.

'Both Gordon and Harvey were killed when we sprang the ambush on the Union wagon and escort. I do not consider that was some act of divine retribution against them. Just as I do not consider I have received punishment from on high because of the order I gave.' His expression and voice became authoritarian again. 'That, lieutenant, is how the deaths of the woman and child came about. In war, such things happen. All I could do in the wake of this particular tragedy was to have the dead laid out in as decent a manner as possible under the circumstances. To await Christian burial in the fullness of time. Are you satisfied, mister? May we now proceed to more pressing matters?'

While Carey was completing the story Sergeant Gilmore was too emotional to finish, Steele reflected on an image of the old man approaching the rear of the house, peering through the window, seeing the corpses of his daughter and grandchild.

Now he came to attention, saluted the dying captain, and responded: 'Yes, sir. I agree. In war, such things happen.'

'Right. Do you have a specific assignement here?'

'No, sir.'

Carey grimaced in response to a wave of pain. Steele's mind was visited briefly by another vivid image. Of Captain Tyson on the brink of death under the wagon far away from here in space and time.

'And I have neither the time nor the inclination to enquire what you and your men were doing here. Until I am no longer able to command, you will take your orders from me. When my time is up, you will take command. Our task here, lieutenant, is to watch for enemy movements on this flank and report them to headquarters. If there is to be a major offensive on this flank we are to withdraw while inflicting as much harm on the enemy as is possible. How many men do you have, lieutenant . . . I don't know your name?'

'Steele, sir. Just two.'

'Damn. It can't be helped. A man has already been despatched to report on this engagement. This will be our command post. Have men positioned in the vicinity to keep watch on further attempts by the Union to sneak troops and supplies along the railroad.'

'Yes, sir.'

'And, Mr Steele . . . '

The Virginian and the sergeant looked back as they turned toward the doorway.

'Have the woman and child buried on this property.'

Steele nodded and went out of the room and the house to do the captain's bidding. Ordered two men to dig a grave large enough to accommodate the bodies of two adults and a child and sent Levy and Trotter back up the embankment to bring down the corpse of the old-timer.

The fighting on Kennesaw Mountain came to an end and an hour later the rain stopped. The grave was finished and the civilians were buried. The dead Rebels were loaded on to the Union ammunition wagon and with just three horses in the traces the vehicle was driven back toward the main concentration of Confederate troops. Three disconsolate Yankee prisoners, their hands tied together with ropes that were lashed to the tailgate, trudged through the mud at the rear of the wagon.

Captain Carey drifted into a coma.

The forward pickets posted by Steele engaged and drove back a patrol of Union soldiers obviously sent to check on the fate of the wagon and escort.

The rain held off and there was no more shooting. The air became oppressive. A mounted messenger rode up to the house with a verbal order. The Union army had abandoned its attempt to take Kennesaw in a full frontal attack and was dividing to outflank the Confederate stronghold on the mountain. Yankees were already well advanced on a swing far to the north-east of where Steele and his men waited, and posed a serious threat to Rebel communications. While a much larger part of Sherman's army was moving on the other flank.

Again General Johnston had decided to withdraw and this time Steele had no option but to become a part in the fall back. For Captain Carey died without regaining consciousness while the messenger was delivering the message.

Back beyond Marietta, the town which was encircled by the mountains. To Smyrna that was the next community south along the railroad.

Confederate soldiers – officers and men – who had been certain the Yankees would be halted and then driven north again at Kennesaw, were embittered and disheartened. From Rocky Face Ridge to here, virtually within sight of Atlanta, Sherman had constantly got the better of Johnston by that most basic of tactics – outflanking. And the Rebel commander and his staff officers seemed to have no answer to this.

So that few of the disgruntled men in grey were impressed by the heavy fortifications at Smyrna that guarded the way to the Chattahoochee River: the final natural obstacle between the Northern army and the prize of Atlanta. Nor did it help to be informed that Johnston's constant fall back from the advance of Sherman was undertaken as part of a well laid plan – to stretch the Union's line of communication and supply so that it was impossible to guard and was therefore open to attack and cutting. For there were no Rebel troops to spare for such assaults.

At Smyrna, the Confederates waited for the Union to launch a Kennesaw Mountain style attack at them. But Sherman had learned by that mistake which had been so costly in Yankee lives. And he veered to the right of the concentration of defences. To bridge the Chattachoochee, known as the Rubicon of Georgia, at the town of Roswell.

With news of yet another flanking move against him, Johnston ordered yet another withdrawal: and the now totally demoralised men under his command were entrenched in what had to be the last ditch defensive positions of the campaign. At Peachtree Creek on the very outskirts of Atlanta – a city almost as vital to the Confederacy as was Richmond. For Atlanta, at the centre of major railroads, was where a large portion of southern cotton was processed. And cotton was the main cash crop that paid for Rebel guns, food, equipment and men.

It was July 9 when Joe Johnston fell back to Peachtree Creek. And eight days later when the Confederate government, in dread of losing Atlanta, made known its dissatisfaction with the commander-in-chief and replaced him with the one-armed and one-legged General John Hood.

Lieutenant Adam Steele was just through with dinner and reading a letter from his father when another junior officer staying at the same small boarding house on Baker Street came in with the news of the replacement. The Virginian acknowledged the information in the same cynical fashion it was given, then went up to his room to re-read the letter from Ben Steele.

It had been mailed at the end of November last year and had thus taken more than seven months to catch up with its addressee. Unlike the few other letters Steele had received from his father during the war, this one touched only briefly on home and business affairs. And it made no mention of Diana. Mostly it was concerned with the writer's conviction that the Union victory at Gettysburg signalled the beginning of the end for the Confederacy. And Ben Steele made much of the address which Abraham Lincoln had delivered at the dedication of the new cemetery at Gettysburg.

Adam Steele's father made no criticisms or recriminations. He wrote in a low key of his feelings toward the inevitable peace and closed by making it clear that if his son so chose to return, he would be welcomed home.

' . . . or if circumstances are such that I cannot be at home, my son, I will be staying at the Palace Hotel in Washington. I will be there or the people there will tell you

135

where I can be found. A letter from you so that I may know whether to expect you or not would be much appreciated.

'Keep safe and well, Adam. What is done is done and cannot be undone. Or forgotten. But forgiveness is within the capability of all of us. And if I am not very wrong, it would appear that in the aftermath of this terrible war, you and I will have little to forgive each other.

'Your loving father.'

The Virginian turned down the lamp by which he had read the letter and stretched out on the bed, on top of the covers, holding the three sheets of paper in both hands to his chest.

For a long time, as evening gave way to full summer night beyond the lace-curtained window of the cramped room, he gazed up at the ceiling: and saw superimposed upon the cracked surface a succession of vivid images. Of men – and here and there a woman – first living and then dead. Comrades and friends who were killed by the Yankees. And Yankees whom he had killed. And as scene after scene of remembered horror showed so clearly in his mind's eye, he sought to lay some of the blame at the feet of his father.

Because Ben Steele was certainly aiding the Union cause. In what manner, his son had no means of knowing. But if the elder Steele had not placed himself on the side of the enemy, it was possible that one or even more of those killings could have been avoided.

Then, at last, the young lieutenant abandoned such a futile exercise. For unless he had the time and facilities to study widely scattered records, it was impossible to establish such a link. And in any event, what his father had written was undoubtedly true: in relation to the havoc wrought and bitterness engendered by the Civil War in some families, the Steeles were fortunate.

What if Ben Steele had been young enough to take up arms for the Union? What if there had been a brother fighting for the enemy? What if one had killed or maimed the other? What if there had been a mother to grieve? How would such families – and there were many of them – face and endure the peace?

Steele sat up, swung his feet to the floor and turned up the lamp. And replied to his father's letter, accepting the invitation to return home. God willing, for the war was not yet over and there was no guarantee that when the peace came he would not have gone the way of those other young men who left Keysville at its beginning. He signed the letter: *Your loving and respectful son, Adam.*

Then he left the boarding house to mail the letter from a city that was still a relatively calm and peaceful one: the long-established civilian population and the influx of military confident it could be defended against the massive Union army camped outside its heavy fortifications.

And having seen sections of the twelve-mile-long circle of redoubts, rifle pits, ditches and timber barricades surrounding the city the Virginian shared in the general belief that the Yankees would never be able to take Atalanta – in a full-scale, all-out attack. But the city was vulnerable to a siege and artillery bombardment if the Union could cut the major railroads which connected it with the outside world.

Already they commanded the Western and Atlantic from Chattanooga. And on that night when Steele sent a letter to his father, Sherman made his first move toward capturing another. The Georgia Railroad that ran east toward Augusta and along which Rebel reinforcements were pouring into the city.

And at three-thirty the following morning Steele's furlough came to an abrupt end when he was roused from restless sleep and summoned to report to a downtown mustering point. Then, an hour later, was in the saddle and riding through the city's eastern defences in a column of four cavalry troops.

It was a warm, clear, moonlit night and the men were in good spirits. Wisecracks were exchanged between the troopers, the artillerymen attending the gun batteries and the infantrymen in the pits and ditches. For, as far as any man below the rank of captain was aware, this was one of the safe sides of Atlanta, since the Yankees were still being firmly held back at Peachtree Creek to the north. And rumour had it that this section of General Joe Wheeler's cavalry corps was being despatched merely to relieve other troopers who had been guarding the Georgia Railroad against the unlikely possibility of a Union attack.

But, as is the way with so many wartime rumours, this one was wrong: as the junior officers and men learned at the abandoned cotton plantation where they made camp a little before noon. There, in the shade of the big house beside the railroad, Major John McNeil flanked by four grim-faced captains made known their orders to the quartet of lieutenants and sixty non-coms and troopers. They, and similar groups of cavalrymen numbering less than one thousand men in total, were being deployed to halt an estimated two thousand Yankee infantrymen who had circled wide to hit the railroad near Decatur and were now pressing west toward Atlanta at a fast pace.

'Two to friggin' one,' Trooper Don Trotter growled to Dave Levy following the order to dismiss after the briefing session. 'That's about what it always seems to be in this lousy war.'

'We've been outnumbered before,' Levy answered with a strained grin. 'And we did okay, ain't that right, sir?'

'We're still alive, that's all we did,' the ugly Trotter countered before Steele could answer. 'Which means we've been lucky, that's all. Luckier than Grady and Brad Barlow, Armistead and Bart Reynolds. All them other guys that didn't make it. But the way I see it, we've been on borrowed

138

time ever since the first Yankee bullets missed us.'

'Hell, that's crap,' another trooper argued. 'It's been proved, man. It don't matter how many times you go into battle, the odds against you gettin' killed stay the same.'

The troopers were heading for a cooking fire in front of a storage barn and, as others in the dozen-strong group joined in the discussion, the Virginian veered away. To go to a live oak growing at the edge of a small pool at the side of the railroad track. Where he sat in the shade of the summer foliage, back resting against the rough bark of the trunk: gazing at the reflection of the big house and its outbuildings on the unmoving surface of the water. Recalling his father's letter and thinking of home and peace as he tossed a small pebble from one gloved palm to another.

For three days the cavalrymen remained at the camp, waiting for the Union infantrymen to come along the railroad toward them: occasionally hearing gunfire to the west to signal probing missions by the Yankees against the Rebel defences of Atlanta. And often in the heat of the day Steele sat under the tree, allowing his mind to wander in the past and conjure up a future while he tossed the pebble and gazed at the reflection on the water of something that bore a certain resemblance to his home.

And he was engaged in just such a sometimes pleasant, sometimes painful, activity when the sound of firing reached to the plantation from the east. And a picket galloped across the cottonfields to report that the enemy was coming: driving before it other Confederate cavalry troops who had failed to halt the advance. By which time Steele had hurled the pebble forcefully into the pool so that the splash and ripples totally destroyed the tranquil image he had uselessly surveyed over the past few days.

All over the camp men were galvanised out of pleasant idleness into tense action as orders were shouted and acknowledged. Horses were saddled, weapons were checked, equipment was packed and then the mounted men assembled into predetermined groups and scattered across the plantation to bide their time in cover.

Steele and ten men, including Trotter and Levy, were assigned to the stable block to the south of the east-facing house. Where they sat astride their horses back from the open doorway which commanded a panoramic view of the cottonfields to the eastward extent of the property where a wooded rise marked the horizon.

During the preparations to join and hopefully halt the running battle, the gunfire had been incessant, growing louder by the second.

Steele pursed his lips. Some men licked theirs. One mouthed a prayer. Another spat a great deal. Everyone sweated and perhaps a few of these were foolish enough to blame the salt moisture oozing from their pores entirely on the heat trapped in the redolent atmosphere of the stable.

'Luck to you, sir,' Levy said tensely.

'And to all of you,' Steele responded, with a glance over his shoulder at the men who were experiencing the same brand of fear as himself.

'Here they come!'

The Virginian faced front again as a corporal with an acne-scarred face blurted the news. And all the men saw the grey-uniformed riders burst from the timber and gallop their horses across the open fields. The front runners crouching low in their saddles while those at the rear exploded wild covering fire.

'Come on, come on,' a trooper urged thickly, speaking aloud the thoughts of every watching man who was willing the fleeing riders to make the safety of the big house and its outbuildings.

Most of them – more than a hundred – were successful. But perhaps a score were hit and sent tumbling amid spraying blood and drafting gunsmoke: falling from their horses to lay inert or to writhe in pain on the stretch of three-quarters of a mile wide ground between the big house and the trees.

For what seemed an agonisingly long time, the men who fired the punishing shots were out of sight. But at last they showed themselves. Wave after wave of blue-uniformed figures running out of the timber. One line halting to fire, then crouching to reload while the line behind ran ahead, fired and crouched.

'Hold steady,' Steele snapped when a trooper in back of him began to curse.

The orders which had come down the chain of command from Joe Wheeler had been clear enough. Based upon the probability that this prong of the Union assault against Atlanta could not be halted. Merely delayed.

The fleeing cavalrymen, weary and afraid, were aware of the presence of reinforcements at the plantation. But, according to the plan, they gave no indication of this. Did not halt their sweating and snorting mounts at the buildings but galloped on beyond. Thus drew the victory-sensing Yankee infantrymen far out into the open cottonfields.

And the forward line was within three hundred yards of the cover in which the fresh troopers were hidden when the signal to charge was blasted by a bugler.

'Give them hell, boys!' Steele roared, and spurred his mount forward: galloping clear of the shade and into the bright sunlight of the afternoon, Spencer carbine resting along his right thigh.

The Union advance had hesitated at the sound of the bugle. Next came to a halt when the men mounting the counterattack were seen. Smartly turned out men astride well-groomed horses. Riding beneath troop pennants that streamed proudly and unscarred from their poles.

Carbines and revolvers cracked countless bullets toward the surprised Yankees and several blue-clad figures pitched to the cottonfields.

The gap between the grey-uniformed riders and the men in blue on the ground narrowed.

Some of the Yankees whirled and began to run for the trees.

Steele saw at least one of these shot by his officer. Then triggered the bullet from his Spencer and saw the enraged captain half-turn and corkscrew to the ground.

The troopers who were now spread out in echelon with the Virginian at the apex had held their fire until he exploded this shot.

They sent a fusillade of lead toward the enemy now, venting the Rebel yell as more blood spurted and screams of fear and pain accompanied the toppling of dead and wounded.

In back of the men who had sprung the surprise counterattack on the Yankees, those who moments before were in full flight wheeled their struggling mounts and added their firepower to the battle.

But the Union lines would not be forced into retreat.

The distance between blue and grey narrowed to nothing. With no time to reload the single-shot carbines, men of both sides drew their revolvers and blasted shots across near point-blank range. And when these weapons were expended of live cartridges, sabres and knives came into play.

All along the three-hundred-yard-wide battle area, men clashed in hand-to-hand combat.

Steele stayed astride his rearing snorting, kicking gelding. Slashing first to the right and then to the left with his sabre. Hearing the din of battle but seeing only those blue-uniformed targets that presented themselves within reach of the viciously wielded sword. Totally ignoring the threat that might be lurking behind or to the sides at the moment he was punishing whatever hapless Yankee was in front of him.

To the neck, the arm, the chest, the back or the skull. The

sabre opened up one gore-gouting wound and sprayed blood into the sunlit air as it whiplashed toward the next target: more often than not the arbitrary twists and turns of the battle-frightened horse deciding in which direction the deadly weapon was to travel.

Never once did the rattle of gunfire cease and then, against the countless reports, a bugle sounded. A frail noise amid the din, but unmistakably sounding recall.

Steele curtailed the slaughter to steady his mount and look around him. There had been a complete overlap of the opposing Rebels and Yankees and he was far behind the forward positions of the Union infantry. As were perhaps thirty other grey-uniformed men still in their saddles – and many who were not. Those who had been unseated or who had chosen to leap to the ground, the better to strike at the enemy.

On all sides of where he turned first one way and then the other in his saddle, the Virginian saw the dead and the wounded – men and animals – littering the bloodstained ground. And even as he surveyed the carnage, it was added to.

And the urge to anger he experienced when he heard the recall bugle was instantly replaced by fear: this as he looked toward the timber and saw more waves of Yankees emerging from the trees. Men being drawn from a seemingly limitless reserve: advancing in the same calm and well-organised manner as those who had been pursuing the fleeing Rebel cavalry just a few minutes earlier.

For a part of a second Steele remained frozen in the saddle, staring through the gunsmoke at the muzzles of the carbines in the Yankees' hands. And it seemed as if every one of them was aimed at him. Then the muzzle smoke spurted. And he felt the slipstreams of bullets coming dangerously close to his flesh. Heard the reports of the volley and only then wrenched on the reins to wheel his mount: thudded his spurred heels into the flanks of the animal and leaned low to gallop away from the mass of guns that had failed to blast a single bullet into him.

He had to veer to left and right so as to avoid running down struggling groups of men and to keep the hooves of the horse from trampling the wounded. And in so doing made it more difficult for any Yankee soldier to take aim and blast a telling shot at him.

He saw the very Jewish-looking Levy had run out of luck – the trooper impaled to the ground with a Union sabre sunk into his belly up to the hilt.

The young trooper with acne had also died on this battlefield: was sprawled across a dead Yankee sergeant with a gaping wound in his throat. The trooper had at least six bullet holes in his back.

The bugle continued to blast, sounding plaintive in its appeal now. The Union attack seemed to gain impetus from the call and the carbine fire was so well ordered it had something of the cadence of Gatling guns spraying death toward the backs of the fleeing cavalrymen.

'Lieutenant, help me!'

Steele recognised the voice of Don Trotter. Then saw the ugly trooper twenty yards in front and to the right. Slowed and steered his horse in that direction. And in closing with the last but one survivor of the former D Troop, the Virginian felt the warm moisture of tears in his eyes.

Trotter was on the brink of death. He lay on his back, his right arm severed at the elbow and he was holding it to his chest with his left hand. Both his legs were trapped beneath the carcase of his horse. There was a bullet hole in his belly.

Agony and anguish emphasised his ugliness.

'Finish me, sir, finish me!' he pleaded as Steele reined in his horse and looked down through the blurring effect of his tears at the pain-racked trooper. 'But write my folks in Mobile I cashed in like a man.'

144

'Sure, feller,' the Virginian answered as he drew the small Remington from his tunic pocket. 'I'll do that for you.'

A bullet snagged his cap. Another snicked the saddle cantle.

Trotter squeezed his eyes tightly closed and blurted: 'We're gonna lose, sir. For sure we're gonna lose.'

Steele leaned low to the side and exploded a shot into the man's head from a range of three feet. The head rolled to the side and was still.

Steele spurred his horse into a gallop again, using the back of a gloved hand to brush the tears from his eyes. Tears that were not just for Trotter. They were for Levy, too. For other men he had known and seen die. At Antienam, Chancellorville, Gettysburg, Lookout Mountain, Rich Mountain and in minor engagements history might or might not record. Men whose names and faces came into his mind and were gone in an instant to be replaced by others.

So many of them that it was awesomely simple for him to think that every man who had served under his command was now dead. And as his mind was attacked by this thought it was immediately replaced by another – that any man whom fate decreed should align himself with Adam Steele was from that moment in the shadow of death's reaching hand.

Then his mind was abruptly empty of memories of the dead and reflections upon his part in their dying: as his subconscious erected a defensive barricade against acceptance of a responsibility too burdensome to be borne by a sane man.

His vision cleared and he felt emotionally drained. To such an extent that as he drew level with the main group of retreating Confederates, he was able to wonder if he would ever again be able to feel anything beyond the physical.

And for the remainer of the war he did not.

Not at Bald Hill, a mile and a half outside Atlanta where Joe Wheeler's cavalry made a valiant and costly stand and twice repulsed the Union before being forced to fall back behind the city's defences.

Not during the days of constant bombardment by Union artillery in which as many innocent civilians as soldiers died under the thousands of non-discriminating shells rained on the besieged stronghold.

Not when he was among those troopers who were the last to leave Atlanta – their mission to destroy factories and railroad rolling stock, ammunition supplies and ordnance that could not be taken by the Confederate army that was once more in full retreat.

Leaving the victorious Union troops free to march into Atlanta on September 2. From where, after a brief respite, Sherman ordered his army again to take up pursuit of the Rebels. But before beginning his march to the sea, the general had the city put to the torch as an example of what he planned to inflict upon the Confederacy until it surrendered. And he was as good as his word.

His objective was the port of Savannah, and in attaining it his more than fifty thousand strong army cut a path of brutal destruction, fifty miles wide and three hundred miles long, through the very heartland of Rebel territory.

Lieutenant Adam Steele was among those who fought grimly to drive back the locust-like viciously vengeful Yankees. And who escaped from Savannah only hours before Sherman's men took the city on December 21.

It was virtually the end. Less than four months before Robert E Lee surrendered the Army of Northern Virginia to Ulysses S Grant at Appomattox Court House.

There were other engagements, before and even after Lee's surrender. But Steele saw no more action. Was sent north in command of a troop escorting a train of ambulance wagons filled with wounded. Bound for Richmond, which

146

was reached on April 1, the day before the Confederate government evacuated the city and nine days before the peace signing at Appomattox.

It was there that he resigned his commission and finished his service to the Southern Cause. Purchased a complete outfit of civilian clothing, a bay gelding and saddle and turned in his army uniform, weapons and equipment.

He rode northward, knowing from a short letter that was sent to him in Richmond that his father would be in a bar on Washington's Tenth Street on the night of April 14 . . . 'waiting to celebrate not the end of anything, but the beginning of a bright future, son.'

The elderly tailor from whom the Virginian purchased his dudish clothing spoke in similariy hopeful terms. And as the young man left his store he called after him: 'May the peace be lasting for all of us, mister!'

For Adam Steele, who was now able to feel a glow of happiness, it lasted until that misty night of April 14. When only those with reason to have hate in their hearts for President Abraham Lincoln had cause to celebrate.

Just the width of a street away from Ford's Theatre where Lincoln was fatally wounded, another man died at the end of a rope. And Adam Steele discovered he was capable of experiencing emotions at the opposite end of the scale from happiness.

Because for him, April 14 marked the beginning of *The Violent Peace.**

THE END OF STEELE'S WAR

* This is the title of the first book in the Adam Steele series.

THE STRANGER: Part Two

ADAM Steele sat throughout the night in a chair on the stoop out front of his store. It was a pleasantly warm west Texas night, but even if the weather had been as cold as it was during the worst of that long Georgia winter of 1863-64, the Virginian would have died from exposure without experiencing the least discomfort.

For as the hours of moonlit darkness slid silently into the past and the false dawn heralded sunrise, the unmoving, impassive-faced man provided undeniable proof that there can exist in human experience the state known as mind over matter.

He had taken just the single drink in Bart Dillon's saloon across the street. Sinking it with one shuddering swallow after the stranger had finished telling him about Lucy. Then he had said just one word: 'Grateful.'

Left the saloon where no one except for the stranger was still drinking and came to his store. Where, in the privacy of the kitchen, he was sick to his stomach: whether caused by the first drink he had taken in many years or the words of the stranger he did not know.

After this he went upstairs to the bedroom he shared with Lucy. There to change his clothing. Donning a lace-trimmed white shirt, a red vest, grey city-style suit, black riding boots and Stetson, silken kerchief and buckskin clothes. All much the worse for wear. Rolled up a pants leg to strap the sheath with the knife into place.

Then he took the Colt Hartford revolving rifle from the closet. The sole inheritance from his father, with its fire-scorched rosewood stock to the right side of which was screwed a gold plate inscribed: *To Benjamin P. Steele, with gratitude – Abraham Lincoln.*

While he sat in the chair on the stoop throughout the night and into early morning, the rifle rested across his thighs: as his mind forgot the present and roved over the distant past. Recalling the closing stages of the war and perhaps reflecting that it would have been better for him if he had been numbered among those many other men who were killed on eastern battlegrounds.

He was unaware of Dillon closing up the saloon. Did not see his fellow citizens of White Rock go their separate ways to their respective homes. Nor notice when a window of the saloon's upper storey was briefly squared with light while the stranger prepared for bed.

The clock in the parlour behind the store struck regularly to mark each hour, but it was not until it chimed ten times that Steele heard it. And curtailed his morbid recollections of the long-gone past: felt a stab of cold anger as he realised he had spent so many hours wallowing in self-pity.

'She's runnin' late,' Bart Dillon said grimly as Steele turned his head to peer out along the south trail. Which showed no sign of the stage from San Antonio which should have rolled into White Rock at ten o'clock.

'Reckon so,' the Virginian answered evenly and surveyed the single street of town. Which normally at this time of day would have been rurally bustling with citizens going about

150

their business.

But this morning there was only the overweight Dillon on the street. Standing some ten feet in front of where Steele sat.With the five-pointed tin star pinned to his shirt front and a gunbelt slung around his waist, a revolver jutting from the holster.

Another man was in sight. The tall and emaciated stranger, showing just his hollow-cheeked, sunken-eyed face and this thin arms and shoulders at the open window of his room above the saloon

Many other pairs of eyes watched the two men out front of the grocery store, but the Virginian could only sense the surveillance for these anxious watchers remained far enough back from their windows to be out of sight.

'I'd hate to have to hang you, Steele,' Dillon said.

'It's not a way I'd like to die, feller,' came the absent reply.

In the window of the store the two flies began to buzz.

Far out along the south trail, something showed against the shimmering heat haze. Bart Dillon saw the slightest of changes come over the face of the Virginian and shifted his attention to the trail.

'You been warned,' he said softly, swung around and strode back across the street. Where, just before he stepped up on to the stoop of his saloon, he directed a tight-lipped glower at the stranger leaning on the window-sill above. Then he took up his arms akimbo stance between the fastened-open batwings.

The team and the Concord it hauled emerged from the shimmering band of heat and showed clearly on the trail. Travelling at a fast but not a headlong pace.

Steele remained seated as he watched the stage approach, billowing an elongated cloud of dust behind it. When it was close enough he recognised the regular driver and shotgun up on the high seat. And heard the elderly man with the reins shouting to him as the stage rolled on to the street, slowing for the stop outside the depot.

'Late on account of your good lady, Mr Steele! Made us stop and keep our eyes tight closed while she changed into the new dress for you!'

His tone was good-humoured and the younger man riding shotgun grinned broadly. But then both men underwent a radical change of mood. When they noticed the deserted state of the street and saw that Steele – as he rose to his feet and stepped down from out of the shade of the stoop awning – looked not at all like a small town grocery storekeeper: had a rifle canted to his shoulder like an extension of the gloved hand fisted around its frame.

The Virginian came to a halt in the centre of the street amid the settling dust as the stage rolled to a stop out front of the depot.

The off-side door swung open and Lucy emerged, looking more beautiful than Steele could remember. She was thirty-two today, but appeared much younger. Three inches over five feet tall, she had a slim build that was almost painfully desirable in the pale green gown that exactly matched the colour of her eyes – hugging closely as it did that portion of her torso it did not reveal above its low neckline. It was obvious that during the unscheduled stage stop she had not merely changed her dress. But had also brushed her long, copper-coloured hair to a fine sheen and repaired whatever damage travelling through the hot morning had wrought to her face.

For perhaps three stretched seconds, while she cautiously stepped from the Concord, taking care that she did not trip, a smile of pure joy was on her face. Then she saw the same scene that had struck apprehension into the minds of the two men up on the stage seat. And her face was suddenly pale, her expression filled with dread as her body became rigid.

'Adam?' she asked huskily after a glance along the street in both directions and she was staring fixedly at the Virginian.

'Looks like the whore she is, don't she mister!' the stranger shouted from the window in the facade of the saloon.

Lucy recognised the voice. Did not look toward the man as she rasped: 'Harry!'

A tear squeezed from the corner of her right eye and cut a moist path down the freshly applied make-up on her cheek.

Steele said evenly: 'He told me you were married in Lousiana. He had a fine business making furniture. You bled him dry. All the time having to buy you dresses like that one. And jewels and expensive perfumes. When he couldn't earn enough to pay for what you wanted, he cheated for you. And when he went to prison because of that, you left. After he was paroled he went looking for you. He found you'd been to a lot of places. Mobile, New Orleans, Charleston, Washington, Baltimore.

'Mostly he got the word from men who'd had to keep buying you the same way he did. Until your trail led back to New Orleans again. And the supply of that kind of man ran out. So you had to become a regular whore in a house on the waterfront. Just to keep your belly filled, let alone pay for high-priced dresses and fancy jewellery.

'He thought he'd reached the end of the trail there, because men don't remember much about every two-dollar whore who gives them a toss. But then he saw a picture of you at some kind of show. And he came here last night and found out times had got so bad for you, you sank to advertising yourself as a mail order bride to any woman-starved man who cared to write you.'

While Steele was speaking, the woman in the new dress continued to stand rigidly on the street at the side of the

153

stage. With tears streaming down both cheeks now, to drip from her jaw to the bared flesh of her upper body.

'Adam!' she wailed, and paused to get her voice under control. 'You never asked. Not once. And I never wanted to know about . . . '

The Virginian, who had not by an inflection of his voice or a line of his expression revealed any emotion to all those who watched and listened, nodded. And interrupted the woman.

'That's the way it was, lady. No questions asked and no lies told. But I'm not casting any stones. Because I reckon I've done worse than you. Never did steal, though. Until you forced me. Another man's wife.'

At the mention of the stranger to White Rock, Lucy turned her head and shuddered when she saw the ugly man at the window. Who fixed her with a stare of depthless hatred for what seemed a long time. Before he drew back from the window. And then the woman took a tentative step away from the stage, half-raising her hands, palms displayed in a gesture of innocence.

'Adam, people change. Especially from when they were young. Lots of folks have done things they're ashamed of. You know I'm not like that anymore. We can start afresh and now you know about how it was it can maybe even be better.'

'Reckon it could be, for us,' Steele allowed as she came slowly toward him. 'But what about your husband?'

Both of them looked toward the saloon as the stranger emerged from it, ignoring what Bart Dillon rasped at him.

The sheriff dropped a hand to drape the butt of his holstered sixgun as the man stepped down off the stoop, pain mixed in with the hatred on his face now.

The buzzing of the green-bodied flies in the grocery store window was the only sound to tremble the hot air of White Rock except for the slow cadence of the stranger's footfalls on the dusty street. Then the only sound when he came to a halt, at one corner of an equilateral triangle with Steele and the woman.

'Mister . . . ' he said.

'Make it a point never to interfere in the affairs of a man and his wife,' Steele cut in flatly.

'Appreciate that,' the stranger said in the same tone.

Drew, cocked, aimed and fired his Smith and Wesson Russian with smooth speed. But no so fast that Steele would have been unable to swing down the Colt Hartford from his shoulder, thumbing back the hammer as part of the same action, and blasting out a shot before the muzzle of the revolver cleared the holster.

Lucy took the bullet through the gentle lower slope of her small left breast. And as she died on her feet and crumpled to the street with an ugly stain spreading across the fabric of the new dress, she displayed an expression of deep melancholy toward Adam Steele.

The flies were silent.

The Virginian felt the threat of tears in the corners of his eyes. He needed to expend an enormous amount of willpower to keep from using the rifle against the man who had killed the woman he loved.

'Damnit, Steele, do somethin'!' Bart Dillon bellowed: as shock was voiced from every building lining the single street.

'I feel like I've been sick for years and I've just been cured,' the stranger said quietly to the Virginian, and began to slide the Russian back in his holster, muzzle still smoking.

'Then I friggin' will!' Dillon snarled.

And leapt across the stoop and down on to the street, clawing awkwardly for his revolver.

The skinny stranger snapped his head around, saw the danger and whirled. Drawing and cocking the gun again.

Dillon's name was yelled and shrieked from along both sides of the street.

The fat man had his gun out, but the hammer was not yet thumbed back.

The thin man was within a fraction of a second of killing him.

The gold plate on the stock of the Colt Hartford glinted momentarily in the strong sunlight. Then smoke spurted from its muzzle.

It was necessarily a back shot, the bullet drilling a hole left of the spine to find the heart, the impact of the lead pitching the man forward before death claimed him. Then he was spreadeagled on his belly in the dust. At the feet of the lawman who raised his eyes from the corpse to direct a look of utter incomprehension at Steele.

The driver and the shotgun clambered down from the Concord. Doors opened and men and women emerged from houses and stores.

'Why, mister?' Dillon asked, his voice shaking with shock as he realised how close he had come to death. 'You let him kill her, yet you save my life?'

The Virginian ejected the spent shellcase and pushed a fresh round into the acrid-smelling chamber. 'A man has to protect what's his own, feller,' he answered. 'The woman never was mine, even if I never did know until last night I'd stolen her from somebody else.'

All White Rock's citizens were on the street now. Mothers holding their children back in doorways while men converged on the scene of the double killing.

'For awhile,' Steele went on, 'this was my town. The people in it my people.'

'Not any more!' a woman called harshly.

Steele glanced around, and saw the elderly banker Riley. He delved into a pocket of his pants, drew out a bunch of keys and tossed them. Riley caught them instinctively.

'Mortgage is outstanding, but you can repossess the store, feller.'

Relief showed in many faces and was heard in the form of expelled breaths here and there in the crowd. Then, before he went to Grant Erland's livery to saddle his gelding and ride away from White Rock, the Virginian crossed the threshold of the grocery store a final time – to reach behind the glass panelled door and turn over the hanging sign. So that it showed . . .

. . . CLOSED.*

* Like this episode in the Adam Steele story. Another will open soon.